FAKE BRIDE'S FIRST LOVE

A Friends to Lovers Romance

J.P. COMEAU

Copyright © 2020 by J.P. Comeau
All rights reserved.
No part of this book may be reproduced in any form or by any electronic or mechanical means, including information storage and retrieval systems, without written permission from the author, except for the use of brief quotations in a book review.

Fake Bride's First Love is a work of fiction. All names, characters, places, and occurrences are the product of the author's imagination. Any resemblance to a person, living or deceased, events, or locations is purely coincidental.

Cover Design by Cover Couture

www.bookcovercouture.com

1

Ginger

The long, emerald dress with a crystal halter-neck strap was too pricey. I should have known better than to visit the most expensive retail store in all of Miami Beach. Everyone knew they only sold high-end, designer clothing. I told myself that I deserved it after all of my hard work. Plus, it was for a special occasion: a party celebrating both my promotion at Lavender Dreams Spa and my earning my MBA.

The second I put it back onto the rack, Guadalupe picked it up and insisted on purchasing it. Not only did she buy that dress, but she also got one for my best friend, Eva.

It was impossible not to give into Guadalupe's natural, maternal ways. Since she and Yuslan had never been able to have children of their own, they often treated us like their daughters. I had no problem with it, either. While I was fairly close to my family, there was something about the way Guadalupe treated her employees that made work more enjoyable. And the fact that she often fed us her amazing Cuban cooking was a bonus.

And that afternoon, both Eva and I were excited to have her cook us lunch. It was a nice change from our standard sushi or pizza takeout. Plus, we had taken the day off of work, so it would just be the three of us instead of chatting in the crowded break room down at the spa. Not that we didn't love our coworkers, but the three of us felt more like a family. If only Margo could have been with us that day too.

Guadalupe let out an audible sigh from behind me as I looked at myself in her full-length mirror. "For the millionth time, Ginger, that will look perfect on you Friday night. That's why I purchased both of your outfits because neither of you could decide on one! Now put it back on the hanger—you're not eating my ajiaco in that thing."

I slid out of the dress and tossed it onto the oversized chair in her dining room.

Eva emerged from the bathroom a few minutes later in her rose-gold dress, which was almost identical to mine except it was covered in sequins.

"Are you sure you don't want this dress, Ginger? We're the same size, and I saw you eyeing it in the store."

I ran my hands up and down the material, remembering how much it stood out on the rack.

"No, Eva. This complements the peachy undertones in your skin, and I think emerald goes better with my auburn hair. You're sweet to ask me, though."

Eva and I had met in college, and her natural, sweet disposition was what had drawn me to her. She was one of the few people who could calm me down using only a few words. She continued to study herself in the mirror, putting her hand on her stomach as Guadalupe reemerged from the kitchen.

"Please don't tell me that you're rethinking your dress, too, Eva! I love you girls, but you drive me crazy sometimes."

The two of us giggled as Guadalupe stood there with her hands on her hips. She owned the spa we worked at but had treated us like her daughters from the day we were hired.

Eva made her way back into Guadalupe's bathroom while I took a seat at the dining room table and started sampling all the makeup.

"The fall line of colors is amazing, Guadalupe. I'm sure the clients will love these at the spa!" I heard her clacking away in the kitchen as she prepared her chicken and potato soup.

"Most of those were picked out by Margo."

"But she's still on maternity leave."

As I swiped a shade of lipstick called Pumpkin Spice onto the back of my hand, Guadalupe came out with two bowls of ajiaco.

"You know how Margo is, Ginger. She's always down at the spa with Joanna."

After placing our lunch down onto her dining room table, she clasped her hands together as she thought about my one-year-old niece. Margo was living with my big brother, Chase, and lived only a few minutes away. She was also my other best friend.

Eva sat down in front of her bowl of ajiaco, eyeing both the soup and the selection of makeup samples with pleasure.

"That color is perfect with your skin tone, Ginger."

I nodded while pushing the makeup off to the side, then digging into Guadalupe's soup. "I think I'll wear it to the party. Guadalupe, this soup is delicious!"

Eva nodded as she dug into her soup too. "I still can't believe you booked the Miami Paramount for the party, Guadalupe. I'm sure nothing from the catering company will be anywhere near as delicious as your cooking."

Guadalupe blushed while sitting down next to Eva at the table with a bowl of soup for herself. "It's the least I could do now that Ginger will be the new accountant at the spa."

"Are you kidding me, Guadalupe? It's my dream job! I get to work with numbers from the beautiful oasis that the spa provides."

Eva giggled while devouring her soup. "Just think about all of the award show after-parties that have been there too."

My body instantly tensed up at the words "award show," but I tried keeping it to myself.

Unfortunately, nothing slipped past Guadalupe. "Spill it, Ginger. What's his name?"

"Nobody, Guadalupe. I'm just enjoying my lunch."

She and Eva smirked at each other and then turned back to me.

"Fine," I said while reluctantly putting down my spoon. "I was just thinking about how Jorge's friend Gavin has been there a few times for those parties."

Of course, Eva's eyes lit up. She was obsessed with movies.

"Isn't that exciting, Ginger? Your boyfriend is friends with a movie star!" Eva had a big mouth.

Guadalupe nearly fell out of her chair, but not because she heard the phrase "movie star." "Boyfriend? Ginger Bowers, why didn't you tell me you were seeing someone? What does he do? Is he alto, oscuro y guapo?"

But before I could correct both of them, Eva—as usual—went off about her love of movies.

"Have either of you seen *House Pharaoh*? It takes place in 19th-century England, and it's about a homeless man who falls in love with a high-class socialite. Oh, it's so romantic!"

I folded both of my hands over my chest and then corrected both of them before they got carried away. "For the record, I am a *single*, independent woman who doesn't have time for a relationship. Jorge is nothing more than a friend. We talk on the phone every Tuesday night, and that's literally all there is to it."

Guadalupe looked suspiciously at me. "Isn't that the guy you danced with at Paris's wedding last year?"

"Yes," I said while staring into my soup.

"And isn't he alto, oscuro y guapo?"

Eva was now giggling to herself, knowing she had gotten under my skin. Ever since I had struck up a friendship with

Jorge, she always wanted to believe that we were more than just friends.

"Yes," I said quietly. "But it's possible to just be friends with a tall, dark, and handsome man."

"Speak for yourself," Guadalupe giggled. "As much as I love Yuslan, I can't control myself whenever I see an alto, oscuro y guapo man." Seeing Guadalupe clutch her heart while reminiscing about all of the handsome men who frequented the spa caused me to relax a bit.

I wasted no time reassuring her that no funny business was going on between Jorge and me. "He's just a friend, you guys. Besides, Jorge lives in Belgium and is sleeping with his business partner, Ria. Does that sound like the kind of guy I want to get mixed up with?"

Eva's right eyebrow turned into a hook. "If he's just a friend, Ginger, then why did you practically hiss Ria's name?"

Even though I had become jealous of Ria, I was dead set on not getting involved with Jorge. Between his history with women and how great my life was going, why would I take that chance? "If either of you thinks that I'm going to pursue a relationship after busting my ass for this MBA and getting the promotion of my dreams simultaneously, then you're crazy. I'm a different woman than I was when I met him."

After we finished our lunch, Guadalupe brought out a tray of miniature cakes that she had baked. My eyes lit up once I saw a passionfruit-flavored one, and my fingers instantly reached for it.

Eva, on the other hand, refused to move her hand. "No, thank you, Guadalupe. I need to lose a few more pounds."

"Like hell you do," she said while sitting down next to her. "Where is this coming from?"

Eva looked at me and then back at Guadalupe. "Anthony dumped me for a supermodel, remember? That never would have happened if I didn't have such wide hips."

Guadalupe leaned forward on the table, a gesture she made whenever she was about to give us some motherly wisdom. "First of all, Eva, I would kill for a body like yours. It's called an hourglass figure, and those hips you're complaining about will attract a fine man just when you least expect it! Second of all, as one of my favorite employees, I will not tolerate you reminiscing about some rat bastard who wasn't worth a second of your time!" And just like that, Guadalupe shoved a miniature purple cake into her mouth, causing Eva to laugh.

As I focused on my miniature peach-colored cake, Eva started talking about how horrible the break-up had been. I knew what Eva was going through all too well. Which was precisely why I didn't want to get sucked down that rabbit hole again. Not after being dumped on Paris's wedding day last year.

Guadalupe was doing her best to cheer up Eva. "Do you think you're ready to date again, Eva? Because there are plenty of hot, single guys in Miami who would trip over their own two feet to have a woman like you!"

Eva just shrugged and looked down at the table. "I'm not

sure, to be honest. But maybe Anthony will see me tagged in pictures online of me dancing with a guy. I might be heartbroken, but I still want to get revenge."

While the two discussed getting back at Anthony, I focused on the makeup, pretending to decide on an eyeshadow color. I was really thinking about Jorge, though. He hadn't been too exciting at Paris's wedding last year, but the two of us had struck up a long-distance friendship after Chase gave me his number. As he told me all about his diamond business from his luxury apartment in Antwerp's Diamond District, I had started to grow quite fond of him.

Get your head out of your ass, woman. Why wouldn't he be like every other guy, who's only interested in sex and the fact that you don't need their money?

Sensing that Guadalupe would pick up on my obvious bow-out of their conversation, I swathed several shades of blush onto my hand.

Nothing romantic had ever happened with Jorge, but secretly I hated that he was sleeping with Ria. What bothered me even more, however, was that she was his business partner. So even if they ever stopped hooking up, she'd always be in his life. Plus, it was only a matter of time before I'd meet her now that he was back in Miami for a while...and living in his penthouse, which was part of the set of condos where I had recently moved after I got my raise from Guadalupe and Yuslan. Of course, that bitch would fly back to check up on him, wouldn't she?

That's what I would do if I were in her shoes.

Guadalupe saw me staring at the eyeshadow samples a little too intensely. "You're thinking about Jorge, aren't you?"

"What? No, I'm just deciding on eyeshadow."

Guadalupe and Eva continued to stare at me, though.

"Are you upset about not having a boyfriend to bring to the party?"

"No, Eva. I don't care about those sorts of things."

Both of them burst out laughing.

Guadalupe was quick to remind me about last year. "I don't think any of us will forget your temper tantrum over not having a date to Paris's wedding and how mean you were to Margo."

I hung my head in shame while thinking about that night and the months that followed. "Yeah, I have some regrets. But I've matured. I'm just really focused on cosmetics right now, you guys. I've never been happier."

Guadalupe cupped my hands with hers. "If you're happy, dear, then why do you look so worried?"

Because I can't stop thinking about Jorge's hooking up with Ria, and I'm worried he won't show up to my party. And I wish I didn't have such jealous tendencies.

"I'm just worried about my dress not zipping up after eating all of these cakes," I said while reaching for another one.

Guadalupe knew I was lying, though. "The universe has a way of working itself out, dear, but just know that there are plenty of alto, oscuro y guapo men who would bend over backward to be with a woman like you. And while you should take this time to focus on your career, remember there will always be something going on in your life that could stop you from falling in love. Don't let that happen, all right?"

I rested my forehead on her hand, thankful to have someone like her in my life.

As the two of them put the soup bowls into the sink, I casually checked my cell phone for Jorge's text messages. We'd spoken on the phone last night, and he reassured me that he'd attend my party. I was secretly hoping for an "I can't wait to see you" message, or maybe a missed phone call.

Nothing.

Please don't stand me up, Jorge.

2

Jorge

As soon as my conference call was finished, I shut down my computer, grabbed my briefcase, and made a beeline for the front door. I had tried to end the call much sooner, but as usual, everyone had a million and one questions. Working in the diamond industry was both enjoyable and incredibly stressful. Some people assumed it was all about the shiny gemstones, but behind the scenes, it was much less glamorous.

The average person walks into a jewelry store, sees a diamond, and gets excited. Someone like myself—a billionaire diamond broker—checks it over to make sure that it's real, asks where it was mined, and asks even more questions that most people wouldn't even think of. But that's why I was so good at my job.

My cell phone went off with several notifications as soon as my hand grabbed the doorknob too.

Can't you people do your job without my having to hold your hand?

Well, they'd have to wait until after I left my trendy apartment in Antwerp's Diamond District and was on my way back to Miami, Florida. Which was, thankfully, thousands of miles away from Ria.

My driver held open the door to the limo, and I wasted no time, sliding inside and closing my eyes. In less than half an hour, I would be flying away from my luxurious but stressful life in Belgium, where I had spent the past year working upward of sixteen hours a day...and sleeping with my business partner on the side. Not that my life in Miami wasn't just as opulent, but there was something mystical about Antwerp's Diamond District.

I poured myself a glass of champagne and allowed the crisp, refreshing bubbles to calm me down. And just as I was settling into my happy place, my cell phone rang.

Nope, let it go to voicemail.

It rang again less than a minute later.

Why can't I get five minutes of peace and quiet?

When it started ringing again, I instantly knew who was calling.

"Yes, Ria?"

"What's with the urgency? Why didn't you tell me that

you were flying back to the States?" Her voice was clipped and full of her usual stuck-up, pretentious attitude.

"We talked about me going to Miami last week. I just hadn't set a date. Do you need something that wasn't covered in our conference call just now? Is that it?"

There was a long pause on her end, and I pictured her long, red nails tapping away on her desk. "Don't bullshit me, Jorge. You stood me up last night too. Do you know how stupid I looked waiting for you in that bar with a bottle of wine and two glasses?"

"I told you that I wasn't sure I could make it, Ria. In fact, I was crystal clear when I said that I'd text you by six o'clock if I could make it. It's not my fault that you went there on your own accord."

"You were talking with *her* last night, weren't you?"

I was about to ask who Ria was referring to, but the emphasis on the word "her" told me—Ginger. "If you're referring to Ginger, one of my best friends, then yes. She and I did speak last night. Why do you care so much?"

"Does she know about me, Jorge?"

I rubbed my temples out of frustration as we got stuck in traffic. "Does she know that I've had a friends-with-benefits situation with my business partner? Yes, Ria, she does know. Now, tell me the real reason you called."

She let out an obnoxious sigh, and I knew she was leaning back in her office chair, closing her eyes and shaking her head. "There will come a day when I say 'no' to your sexual advances, Jorge."

"*My* sexual advances? Are you kidding me right now?" I ignored the look of shock from my driver in the rearview mirror.

Oh, please. Like you didn't know.

"So, how long until you get back to Belgium?"

"I don't know, Ria, and it won't matter because everything I do can be done remotely. Just focus on running the business on your end, and I'll do the same from mine. Everything will be fine."

"You're so selfish, Jorge. Aren't you interested in how I found out that you were going back to Miami?"

A massive lump formed in my throat as I realized that she was right. The only person who knew was my secretary, and she was too damn trustworthy to have told Ria. The company-wide email she sent out merely stated that I'd be out of town for an indefinite amount of time, but business would continue as usual.

I refused to give in to her bullying tactics, though. "Not at all, Ria. Now, if you'll excuse me, I have a plane to catch."

I hit the "end call" button as soon as she started to speak again. Then, I nodded to my driver as the traffic eased up.

About thirty minutes later, I was flying high above the Atlantic Ocean in my private jet, doing my best to forget all about Ria. Deciding that it'd be a long flight, I gave my best friend, Gavin, a call.

The sound of people chatting blared into the phone when he picked up. "Hey, man! Hang on a second, let me go someplace quieter." I adjusted my gold Rolex while waiting for him to return, admiring the diamond detail.

"All right, there we go. What's going on, man?"

"Nothing, but it sounds like you're pretty busy. Did I catch you at a bad time?"

"Not at all, but you sound a bit under the weather. Is it stress or problems with women?" Gavin knew me all too well.

"It's Ria problems, man. That woman is driving me insane."

"How many times did I tell you not to get involved with her? Not only do you work with her, but she's your freaking business partner!"

I closed my eyes, realizing he was right. But the sex was good and, well, don't we all have needs? "I know, but she said she was fine with a friends-with-benefits situation. How could I know she'd get so attached?"

"Women always get attached in those situations, Jorge. It's just how they're wired. And I've never liked Ria, either."

"You've never even met her."

I overheard him place a coffee order to one of his assistants.

"She's the kind of person you can judge before meeting them. Some of the things she's said just don't sit well with me."

"Can you give me an example?"

The stewardess brought me a bottle of champagne, which I quickly popped open and started sipping.

"Whenever a large sum of money pours into your business,

didn't you tell me you always end up being a few thousand dollars short at the end of the month? That alone bothers me, especially since she handles the finances of your firm."

I took in what he was saying and knew he wasn't wrong. "Well, it's a large business, so I'm sure it went somewhere and she always has an answer for it." I didn't want to admit to Gavin that, yes, I was also suspicious of her taking money. "But as far as our relationship goes, she used to be cool about it until recently."

"That's because you've been getting closer to Ginger, man. She's direct competition to Ria because regardless of what she says that woman wants you all to herself. And really, can you blame her? You're the perfect catch for a woman looking for someone to spoil her."

Gavin was right, and there was no way in hell that I'd ever date a woman like Ria. She was bossy, controlling, and extremely demanding. It was an ideal personality to have in a business partner but not in a romantic one.

"But I keep telling her that I don't want to be serious."

"Oh, come on man. Do you say this before or after the two of you have sex? Because women view sex as a sign of commitment. So while your mouth says one thing, the brain between your legs says something entirely different."

I finished my glass of champagne and quickly poured another one. "Let's change the topic because the mere mention of her gets under my skin. Any new movie contracts coming up?"

"There are a few in the works, but I'm skeptical about one

of them. My agent tells me it's bound to win an award, but the female lead reminds me too much of my ex-girlfriend, Melissa."

"You mean the mother of your daughter? That Melissa?"

Gavin said, "thank you" to someone, and I knew he was taking his sweet time returning to our conversation. "Yes, that one. Anyway, our intimate scenes together will bring up too many painful memories, and I don't need the added stress...or the effect it might have on my performance. I'm thinking, I might have to pass on this one."

"You can't pass on a movie that has a good chance of winning an award! Don't you want that for your mantle?" My hands clung to the armrest as we hit turbulence, which thankfully didn't last too long.

"At what price, though? There is no guarantee I could actually deliver what the director is looking for... there's no award in that."

"Good point."

"Speaking of women, are you going to Ginger's party this weekend?"

"How did you find out about it? First, Ria finds out that I'm flying back to the States without anyone telling her, and now you found out about Ginger's party."

Gavin chuckled into the phone. "Relax, man. Chase posted something about it on his social media, so I assumed you were going."

I wanted to come off as nonchalant as possible because I had never been one to get emotionally invested in a woman.

As a diamond broker, women were always throwing themselves at me, and all it took was something sparkly to seal the deal. But there was something about Ginger that kept pulling me back, even though we were only friends.

"That's one of the reasons I'm going back to the States, actually."

"I knew—"

"And before you say, 'I knew it,' no, we are not more than friends. But she just graduated with her MBA, plus she got a massive promotion at the spa. I would fly back if any of my other friends were celebrating those accomplishments too."

"Mmm-hmm."

"Whatever," I said while feeling the champagne give me a buzz. "Anyway, I should probably let you go. This champagne is starting to get to my head, and I could use a good nap."

"All right, man. Let me know how your girlfriend's—I mean *friend's*—party is this weekend."

I chuckled while hanging up the phone, then leaned back and fell asleep for the rest of the flight.

The pilot had to wake me up once we had landed several hours later, and I happily took the latte from the stewardess while getting off the plane. The hot, humid air hit my face as I made my way through the executive airport, walking until I saw my driver waiting for me while holding the door open to the limo.

It felt good to be back in Miami, and I took in all of the surroundings as we made our way to my penthouse. As much as I loved my apartment in Antwerp, the penthouse felt more like home to me. A furniture designer had made my couch, which was a mix of contemporary and vintage. I had fallen asleep on it numerous times because it was so damn comfortable. Plus, I had a mini bar in almost every room.

Once I arrived home, I quickly looked over at Ginger's condo to see if she was there. Her car was gone, which meant she was either at work or spending time with the girls.

Relax. You'll see Ginger this weekend.

I opened the door to my penthouse, threw my suitcases onto my bed, and headed straight for the shower. I loved a hot, steamy shower after a long flight. I closed the glass door and allowed the water to drench my body. After washing myself from head to toe, I wrapped a towel around my waist and plopped onto the sofa.

Just as I finished the rest of my latte, which had started to get cold, my cell phone went off. Usually, I'd let it go to voicemail after such a long flight, but I thought it might be Ginger. Maybe she saw me walking inside right as she was pulling into the parking lot.

It was Ria.

As soon as it stopped ringing, I turned it off and chucked it onto my bed.

What have I gotten myself into?

3

Ginger

There must have been several hundred guests at my party that night, which far surpassed my expectations. When I asked how many people Guadalupe and Yuslan had invited, she insisted that I not worry about anything other than having a good time. I pleaded with her to keep it low-key and only invite my family and friends, but of course, she didn't listen to me. Nearly every client of Lavender Dreams Spa was there to celebrate my MBA and promotion.

Everyone in Miami Beach loved Guadalupe and Yuslan, and it showed.

Even though Miami was a pretty large city with plenty of spas for people to choose from, Lavender Dreams Spa was known as one of the top five in the area. We catered to everyone from regular, blue-collar people to celebrities who either lived in Miami or were in town visiting. And while I didn't see any famous people that night, I did notice a few managers of actors who I had every intention of meeting one day. That was one of the perks of working in that type of industry.

While I was thrilled to see so many people there celebrating with me, I focused on Margo's massive engagement ring. "I can't believe you two are getting married! When did Chase propose to you?"

Margo's eyes lit up as Eva and I studied it. "This morning, over pancakes and while I was feeding Joanna!"

Eva's eyes bugged out as she looked up at Margo. "Are you serious, Margo? He proposed over pancakes? Why does that sound so romantic?"

I knew my brother all too well, though. "That doesn't surprise me one bit, guys. Chase has always been an 'in the moment' kind of guy, and I bet he saw you feeding Joanna and just knew it was the right time."

Eva ran her fingers over the stones, no doubt thinking about how her ex-boyfriend used to always say that she was "the one." "You're so lucky to have found someone, Margo. I'm so happy for you."

Margo and I knew better than to bring up her ex-boyfriend, though. "You and Chase were meant to be together," I said as Eva took a long sip of her champagne and eyed the room, probably looking for a guy to flirt with.

We'll make that jerk wish he'd never broken up with you.

Tears came to Margo's eyes as she smiled and nodded at me. "It was such a passionate speech, you guys. But I don't want this to take away from your night. That was my first thought after I accepted his proposal."

I wrapped my arms around Margo's neck and pulled her in for a tight hug. "Margo, the fact that we're going to be sisters-in-law is all I care about right now!"

As her enormous ring dug into my shoulder, I overheard one of our regular client's screech while rushing toward us. "Margo, you're engaged! Oh, honey, isn't that wonderful? I'm so happy for you!"

Alona was an over-the-top, eccentric, middle-aged woman with a heart almost as pure as Guadalupe's. She often referred to us as her daughters too. I embraced it, although her shrieks often went right through my head. She was the reason I started keeping ibuprofen on hand.

As Margo told her all about the proposal, I casually sipped champagne while looking at the door. People were still making their way into the party, but there was no sign of Jorge. I tried acting nonchalant by smiling at people standing near the door, pretending as though I were simply paying them some attention.

And I had every intention of staying in that spot until Yuslan tapped me on the shoulder. "Would you care to dance, dear?"

I couldn't turn down a dance with a man who was like a

father figure to me, especially after he went to such great lengths with the party.

The two of us danced around the ballroom while the live band played, his hands resting on my hips as Guadalupe watched with a smile on her face. I let him lead, even though I craned my neck every time he turned us around and I was facing the doorway.

My stares didn't go unnoticed by him, either. "What's his name?"

I give up. "Nothing gets past you or Guadalupe, does it?"

Yuslan flashed his usual 'I know you too well' smile at me. "So, what's his name?"

Just as I was about to tell him the whole Jorge story, someone tapped me on the shoulder. I turned around and stopped dead in my tracks. There was Jorge, smiling down at me and looking sexy as hell.

"Jorge, you made it!"

The two of us hugged as Yuslan let go of my hips.

Ever the gentleman, Jorge, acknowledged what he had done. "I'm so sorry, but would you mind if I cut in? I'm Jorge, by the way."

"Yuslan," he replied while shaking his hand and smiling. "And no, not at all."

I gave Yuslan an apologetic look, but he had no problem passing me off to Jorge. He winked at me and then made his way over to Guadalupe, who looked ravishing in her cobalt-blue sequin dress, and the two of them started dancing.

"I'm so happy you made it," I said as Jorge took my hands.

We started dancing across the ballroom, and for a few minutes, all we could do was stare into each other's eyes. It was as though time stood still and our year-long friendship had culminated into something a bit more in that moment. I snapped myself out of it when I saw Margo comforting Eva in a corner, though.

Eva was sobbing into her hands as Margo rubbed her shoulders. The poor girl had been through enough. After catching explicit text messages on Anthony's phone, she had confronted him, and he told her everything. The worst part was that Eva had repeatedly told us that she knew he was "the one" from the moment their eyes had locked.

"Of course I made it, Ginger. Why would you doubt me?"

"Well, you did have to come all the way over from Belgium. That's a far cry from Miami."

His grip on my hips became a little bit tighter, and it started to feel as though the room were closing in on me. There was an undeniable heat between us that I kept trying to push away, but it felt like a magnet. All of our late-night conversations had led to that moment, and I started to rethink my feelings toward him.

"It was worth it, though. You're just as beautiful as the last time I saw you, by the way."

I could feel my cheeks turning a deep, rosy hue as I took in his compliment. "Thank you. You don't look so bad yourself." *Oh, God. That was awful!*

Thankfully, Jorge chuckled at my bad joke. "I'll take that as a compliment."

"I mean—"

Jorge put his finger to my lips and shook his head. "Don't even worry about it, Ginger. I know it's always a bit awkward after you've been chatting with someone remotely, and then you finally get to see them in person. I'm just delighted to be here."

We started dancing again, and this time he pulled me closer to his chest. His cologne was intoxicating, and if it weren't for his strong hands holding me in place, my knees would have given out. I looked over at Eva, who was no longer crying. In fact, when our eyes met, she gave me a cheesy thumbs-up.

I rolled my eyes while smiling at her, knowing she had nothing but good intentions. My only concern was someone seeing her and telling Jorge because, as much as I was drawn to him, I intended to stay single for the next several years. I had spent the last few years chained to a desk whenever I wasn't at work, doing my best to earn nothing but straight *A*s. Now it was my time to sit back and enjoy life, before settling into another romantic relationship.

As the band announced they'd be taking a short break, Jorge walked me over to a nearby table and sat down. "I meant it when I said that you're beautiful, Ginger. That emerald dress really brings out your thick, auburn hair."

Yes! I knew I made the right choice.

I pretended to wipe something off my dress, and when I looked up, Guadalupe was smiling at me.

"Thank you, that's what I was hoping for when I picked it

out. Although, you'll have to thank Guadalupe. I told her it was too much money, but she insisted on buying it for me."

"Well," he said while leaning forward and taking both of my hands, "I'll be sure to do that. In the meantime, however, that wrist looks awfully lonely."

I glanced down at both of my wrists to see what he was talking about, and then it hit me.

Dammit! I knew I should have worn a bracelet!

"I was so worried about looking good for tonight that I completely forgot about jewelry! Well, except my pearl earrings. But I didn't go with a necklace because—"

Jorge put his finger to my lips again while his other hand reached into his pocket, only to reemerge holding a diamond tennis bracelet. He took my left hand and wrapped it around my wrist, clasping it shut. My mouth fell open as I held it up to the massive crystal chandelier dangling above us, mesmerized by how much the bracelet glittered.

"It sparkles with your eyes, Ginger."

"Jorge, you really shouldn't have gotten me a diamond tennis bracelet! This must have cost you a fortune!"

He shrugged while reaching for my hand, then led me back onto the dance floor. "It's the least I can do for my friend on such a special occasion. Besides, what else are diamond-broker friends good for?"

I giggled while resting my head on his shoulder, positioning it so that I had a perfect view of the tennis bracelet. It was easily the most beautiful piece of jewelry I had ever owned. But the more I stared at it, the more I understood it for what it most likely was: a way to win me over, either for dating or just sex.

I refuse to end up like Eva, sobbing uncontrollably over some guy.

So, I straightened my shoulders and looked him dead in the eyes. "Well, I can't thank you enough, Jorge. It'll go so well with some of my new work clothes. After being promoted, I figured it was a good excuse to go shopping."

He picked up on what I was doing, which only seemed to excite him.

As I droned on about my career goals, the two of us spent the rest of the evening dancing around the ballroom. I tried to break away a few times to speak with family and friends, but Jorge was his usual magnetic self. Not once did he look at any of the other women, not even the ones who were wearing significantly more expensive dresses than myself. He planted all of his attention on me.

And that made him even more attractive.

By the time the party was over, I had both a strong buzz and sore feet. "Well, looks like I'm not driving home tonight."

Jorge tilted his head as he wrapped his arm around my waist. "I'll gladly drive you home, Ginger. Besides, we live at the same property, remember?"

By the time his Bentley pulled into our parking lot, my head was spinning like crazy, and I was riding a major high. The entire evening had been an enormous success. Guadalupe and Yuslan had pulled the party off without a hitch, and everyone seemed to have had a good time. Margo and Eva spent most of the evening discussing her upcoming wedding between Eva's sobbing, and I had spent nearly all of it pressed up against Jorge.

He walked me to my condo and made sure that I got inside. And just as I was about to close the door, he brought my hand to his lips and kissed it. "I'll call you Tuesday evening."

All I could do was smile while shutting the door, and as it clicked shut, I realized my head was spinning even more so than before.

It must be from all of the champagne. Yeah, just too much champagne.

4

Jorge
Four Days Later

There were many perks to working from home: staying in my pajamas, not having to beat rush-hour traffic, and not having to smell other people's food wafting from the break room. One of the worst culprits was my secretary. While she was a hard worker and one of the few employees I'd trust with my life, she ate fish nearly every damn day. Her excuse about the horrid smell of her microwaved salmon was its health benefits, but I was close to instituting a no-fish policy in the office.

That was what was running through my mind as I powered up my laptop, the only aroma being my Colombian coffee and a blueberry bagel. But my favorite benefit, however, was not having people know that I was at my desk. Whether it was in Antwerp or Miami, employees flooded my office within seconds of my sitting down. And nothing had been so crucial that my secretary couldn't have taken care of it, had they only gone to her in the first place.

Once I logged onto the network, I groaned at the number next to my email icon: over a two-hundred messages were waiting for me. The only ones that actually got through to me were those that my assistants couldn't handle since they had access to my primary account. My secondary email was so private that only a handful of people even knew of its existence.

I overheard some workman talking in the hall outside my door. They were repairing the pool nearby, which was fine by me. Working so many hours didn't give me nearly enough time to go swimming, which was one of my favorite hobbies. And I couldn't help but wonder what Ginger would look like in a sexy bikini, both of us drinking margaritas on the beach or beside the rooftop pool. The thought alone caused me to get a bit hard between my legs, so I shook my head and focused on work.

There was far too much on my plate to be getting sidetracked.

One of the organizations was the De Veers Diamond Group. I had inherited a part of it from my father, and it dealt with several diamond mines in Africa. My eyes gravitated to that email first. Since I had such a personal investment in it, I quickly read over their concerns.

Long story short, the miner's union was demanding an increase in wages. The person who handled that for me was Ria, so I shot her a message on our interoffice communicator. Her status was available, and she usually replied quickly. But there was not even a peep from her that morning.

So, I pulled out my cell phone and sent her a text message. When several minutes passed and she still hadn't gotten back to me, I grumbled to myself while calling her office phone, dreading her voice so early in the morning. It merely rang and rang, then went to her voicemail.

"Ria, it's Jorge. I'm forwarding you an email from De Veers Diamond Group. It's about the laborers working in the mines in Africa. They're demanding an increase in wages, so please take care of it."

I poured myself another cup of coffee while awaiting her response. In the past, she'd always been excited about talking with me.

Nothing.

So, I called her cell phone and, of course, got her voicemail.

"Ria, it's Jorge. I find it hard to believe that you're not available. Anyway, I just sent you an email from De Veers Diamond Group. Message or call me back to verify you're taking care of it."

My personal, vested interest in the diamond group was too big not to address the issue immediately. I stood to lose millions of dollars if it weren't taken care of because those miners were paramount to our operation. So, when I hadn't heard from her in over an hour, I sent my own damn reply authorizing her to start negotiations with their union leader ASAP. Then I spent the rest of the day wondering what the hell Ria was doing and praying the workers wouldn't just walk out without agreeing to start negotiations.

I breathed a sigh of relief when, at fifteen minutes to five, De Veers emailed me back, confirming they agreed to continue mining operations while negotiations got underway.

Ria never got back to me.

Frustrated at my poor choice of ever sleeping with Ria, I poured myself a glass of pinot noir and thought about Gavin's comments. I never wanted to admit it to him, but I really was concerned about all of that missing money. Since I was a billionaire, at first, I had just considered it chump change and shrugged it off. But if Ria were embezzling thousands of dollars—or more—it would only be a matter of time before she grew bigger balls and tried to take millions. And besides, embezzlement was a crime, and I didn't want a criminal for a business partner.

After a turkey sandwich and baked potato, I decided to discuss it with Ginger.

"Hey," her sweet voice said into the phone. "I just finished dinner. How was your day?"

"Pretty busy as usual. I just finished dinner too."

"Anything exciting?"

I stared at the crumbs on my designer dinner plate. "Turkey, Swiss cheese, lettuce, bacon, and pesto on whole wheat. Oh, and a baked potato with butter and sour cream."

"Someone's getting all fancy."

I chuckled while allowing her warm, velvety voice to calm my nerves. "Well, it would have tasted better if you were here."

"Yeah, right. So, did anything big happen at work?"

I suddenly wondered if telling her about the whole Ria ordeal was a good idea.

She's your friend, dammit, and friends help each other out.

"Funny you should mention that because I was asked to handle a situation at the diamond mines in Africa. But only because my business associate, who normally takes care of that stuff, was MIA."

"You mean Ria?" Her voice tensed up when she said Ria's name.

"Yeah, the same one I've, well, you know. I mean, not anymore. Anyway, I think Ria is avoiding me because I called it off with her. And to make matters worse, I also think she's embezzling funds from our business."

"Jorge, you can't be serious! Embezzlement is a serious crime! Have you had anyone audit the books for you?"

Just ask her, dammit. The worst thing she can say is "no."

"Actually, and I completely understand if you can't or don't want to, but—"

"I'll gladly look over your books and do a quick audit," she interjected.

I grinned from ear to ear. "Are you sure? I know it's asking a lot of you, but it's hard to find someone I can trust."

"Don't even worry about it. This is what I love to do."

I eyed my laptop, wondering how long it'd take me to give her all of the documents. "Any chance you could come over tonight?"

"Since we're literally neighbors, I can manage that. What time?"

"Now?"

"See you in five minutes."

After quickly changing into a pair of khakis and a blue polo shirt, I grabbed another wine glass just as Ginger rang my doorbell. She was wearing a form-fitting, red halter dress, which showed off her curves while teasing me just enough about what was underneath. And the diamond tennis bracelet I had given her was sparkling on her wrist.

"Ginger, you look—I mean, come on in. I really appreciate your helping me out."

"No problem."

Her matter-of-fact attitude was the polar opposite of Ria's, who never shied away from flirting with me. I was a man who appreciated the chase, and the more Ginger resisted me, the more I wanted her.

She's just a friend.

"Why don't you come into my office," I said while pouring her a glass of wine.

She sat down across from me as I pulled up the necessary documents. "If it's easier for you, you can just email them to me."

"That's probably a good idea, although I should forewarn you—it's a lot. I need someone to go back to when Ria joined my business, so I'm afraid I'm asking too much of you."

She waved her hands in the air at me. "I enjoy this kind of stuff, so I'm actually pretty excited to get started. Anything you want to tell me before I dig in?"

Yes, I want to tell you how sexy you are and that I need to be inside of you sooner rather than later.

"Only that she's a conniving woman who I never should have gotten involved with."

"Well, don't be too hard on yourself. Based on what you've told me, it sounds like Ria was the one making all of the passes."

"That's true."

Ginger took a long sip of her wine as a few awkward moments passed. Her eyes slowly moved up and down my body as I leaned back in my chair, and I realized that my erection was reasonably visible. Ginger looked at it, and I quickly sat back up, pulling myself forward so it was hidden under the desk. "I mean, can you blame her?"

I could feel my balls getting more cumbersome the longer she stared at me. "What do you mean?"

She gulped down the rest of her wine and rested the empty glass on my desk. Our eyes locked for a few minutes until I could no longer help myself. I allowed them to go farther south, toward her full, voluptuous breasts whose nipples were hardening underneath her dress. I licked my lips as Ginger slowly slid off one of the straps, allowing it to fall down to her left elbow.

And then she did the same to the right strap.

I remained silent while standing up, made my way over to her, and pressed my lips to hers without hesitation. We passionately kissed as she quickly slid off my polo, then ran her nails all along my chest. I picked her up, wrapping her legs around my waist, and then carried her into my bedroom. As she fell on top of my California king-sized fluffy white comforter, she shimmied out of her dress until she was only wearing a black G-string.

Within seconds I was naked, my hot, writhing body on top of hers as we rolled around. My erection pressed against Ginger's lace G-string until neither of us could take the heat. She grabbed my hand and used it to slide off her panties until her swollen pussy pushed up against my cock.

"Are you sure, Ginger?"

She nodded while shoving me onto my back, and then straddled my cock, sliding it all the way inside of her as both of us moaned with pleasure.

Being inside of Ginger was better than I could have ever imagined it'd be, her warm, velvet opening massaging my shaft as we rocked back and forth. She leaned forward, pressing her bosom against my chiseled abs while squeezing my shaft from within. Her skin was silky smooth and felt so soft against my rugged, rough hands.

"Oh, Jorge!"

"Ginger! I have to admit, I've been fantasizing about this."

"Me too."

Both of us closed our eyes as we made passionate love in

my bedroom. Even though I'd developed a secret crush on her and suspected that she felt the same way about me, I still had reservations about having sex. But there we were, both of our bodies becoming one as we released a year's worth of pent-up, sexual frustration.

Ginger flipped onto her back, allowing me to climb on top and plow deep inside of her. We remained focused on one another as I pumped away, sensing that our orgasms would coincide. We stared deeply into each other's eyes as it happened, her legs shaking uncontrollably as my seed mixed with hers and became one.

I rolled over onto my back, the two of us panting heavily, gasping for air. The whole ordeal hadn't lasted more than a few minutes. That didn't sit well with me. "Ginger, I normally last a lot longer. Did you—"

"Yes, Jorge, that was unbelievable." She was still struggling to catch her breath.

I wrapped my arms around her, realizing that no matter how hard we tried to fight it, our sexual chemistry was too strong to deny. And as someone who'd never been in a serious relationship before, that scared the shit out of me.

5

Ginger

My stomach growled louder as it got closer to noon. I was tempted to take an early lunch, but my workload was bigger than I'd anticipated. Doing the accounting for Lavender Dreams Spa was more intense than I'd expected, but at least I was in my own office with a breathtaking view of the ocean.

I opened my desk drawer, ransacking it for a protein bar of some kind. But all I could find was a package of crackers from the soup I'd had the other day. I made a mental note to put some snacks in my desk. And while I considered venturing out into the break room, knowing Guadalupe had probably brought in some of her baked goods, I decided against it. If I kept eating everything she baked, I'd go up a size and have to buy a new wardrobe.

That was exactly what I told Guadalupe every time she brought me one of her miniature cakes.

I turned around in my chair to look at the crystal-blue water and the waves crashing against the beach, thinking about how thankful I was for everything. I loved my job, where I lived, and had the best friends a girl could ask for. Thanks to careful planning, everything in my life was going in the right direction.

Plus, I got to have sex with Jorge last night.

I had told myself that I wouldn't sleep with him, but who was I kidding. After a year's worth of sexual tension building between us, it just seemed like the next step in our relationship. Especially, since he had broken things off with Ria.

Actually, Jorge had no reason to invite me over there for anything other than sex since he knew everything could be handled via email. That's why it had taken me fifteen minutes instead of five to get to his place. I had ripped off my pajamas and chose the sexiest halter dress I owned. And I knew Jorge had been home all day, too, because his car had never left the parking lot. Which meant that he was probably working in pajamas too. But when I got there, he looked pulled together in that polo and khakis.

He knew what he was doing.

I shook my head and went back to work, refusing to allow myself to get sidetracked. But every time I tried calculating numbers, all I could think about was how good it felt to have Jorge buried inside of me.

God, I could have fallen asleep in his arms.

By the time I looked up, it was five minutes to noon, Margo's and Eva's voices boomed down the hallway. I planned on picking up something from a drive-thru and eating it by the beach, but apparently, my best friends had other plans.

Margo popped her head into my office first. "Is it all right to come in? I have a surprise!"

"Of course, come on in. What's the surprise?:"

Eva walked in behind her, carrying a large tray of sushi from our favorite Asian restaurant.

"The celebration continues with some California, cucumber, and dragon rolls! How about we eat outside today? The weather's perfect, plus they're working on the building across the street and the guys are hot," Eva said.

We giggled as the three of us walked outside, sitting down on one of the many picnic benches next to the spa.

"There's nothing wrong with a little bit of scenery while we eat, is there?" I asked.

Eva nodded toward the diamond tennis bracelet on my left hand. "Have you been wearing that since the party?"

"No, I take it off when I shower. Besides, Jorge probably spent a fortune on it and it *is* beautiful, so I don't want to lose it."

Margo winked at me while eating a cucumber roll. "Your wrist is glistening, and the smile on your face is telling. Did something happen between you two?"

My cheeks turned a deep shade of red, and I planned on chalking it up to the humidity. But even I wouldn't have bought that lie. "I'm helping him out with his business, but I'd do that for any friend. Accounting stuff, nothing too exciting."

Eva saw right through my lie too. "Tell us what happened, Ginger, and don't skimp on the details!"

I tried focusing on my sushi, not wanting to tell anyone what had happened. For all I knew, Jorge and I hooking up was a one-time thing. He had an awful history with women, and I didn't want to get sucked down the relationship rabbit hole again.

But I caved in and gave them the details. "You can't tell anyone else, though, especially Chase. Last night we, well, you know."

"You had sex with Jorge?"

The construction workers across the street glanced over at us.

"Shh, Margo! If those guys can hear it, you know damn well everyone in the spa can!"

Margo just shook her head while smiling from ear to ear. "I knew it! I'm telling you, Ginger, Jorge will be more than just a fling!"

Eva's eyes lit up with excitement as she leaned across the picnic table. "Oh, this is so exciting! Do you think Jorge is the one?"

"Of course he's the one," Margo said while grinning at me. "They've spent the past year talking on the phone every week, then he flies all the way from Belgium for her party, surprises her with a diamond tennis bracelet, and then makes love to her!"

I held up my hands while shaking my head back and forth. "First of all, both of you are crazy. I have every intention of keeping my relationship with Jorge on a strict friendship level."

Eva squinted at me. "I think you mean friends-with-benefits level, Ginger. Because friends don't sleep with each other, but friends-with-benefits do."

I shrugged while reaching for another sushi roll. "Whatever you want to call it, that's what we are, all right? Look, my life is finally on track, and I refuse to get sucked into a romantic relationship. Besides, I don't think Jorge is that type. We're just friends who happen to be attracted to each other."

"If you say so," Eva quipped while glancing over at the construction guys again.

I tried changing the subject to focus on Eva for a bit. "So, how do you like being the manager of the spa now?"

"It's all right. I can see why you were frazzled at times, though. It can be a bit overwhelming trying to manage everything at once, but Guadalupe says that I'm doing a great job."

"You know," Margo said while pointing her chopsticks at me, "there's a good chance that you're the reason Jorge called it off with Ria."

I wanted to tell her to lay off the Jorge talk for a while but was interested in why she felt that way. "Why would you say that?"

"Well, he used to tell Chase how much he hated her personality. But, well, she was good in bed and she had experience in the diamond brokerage business. Anyway, once you two started talking regularly, Chase noticed that he rarely mentioned Ria anymore. Chase said, the only time Jorge mentioned her name was when he was complaining about her."

I couldn't help but smile. Just knowing that I may have had something to do with the dissolution of Jorge's relationship with Ria put a little more pep in my step for the rest of the day.

I spent the afternoon hunched over my desk, doing my best to breathe in the fresh lavender that was pumped continuously throughout the spa. Yuslan said it was a great way to naturally relax people as soon as they came inside, and it also worked well at keeping the staff calm. Their secret was using actual lavender, not some fake, synthetic oil. When clients walked inside, they were hit with the scent, and many said they looked forward to their appointments for that reason alone.

By the time five o'clock came around, I was mentally exhausted. But I had promised Jorge that I'd look over his books, so I grabbed a salad to go from a nearby restaurant and headed home where I promptly got to work.

Jorge wasn't kidding when he said there was a lot to go over. Everything he had sent me went back to the beginning of his business, and it didn't take me long to find some discrepancies. Within a month of Ria's joining his company, I noticed several thousand dollars per month was lost, and unaccounted for. She had done an excellent job of keeping track of their expenses, but it was obvious Ria never expected Jorge to run the numbers. She had altered the bank ledger to indicate reconciliation discrepancies. Those entries made the books seem to balance, masking the loss to only the trained eye.

Which was where I stepped in.

I tried to focus on the math, but my mind kept drifting off to the two of them in bed. I was overcome with jealousy as I pictured Jorge on top of her, pumping away as he had done with me the night before. And he had made it perfectly clear to her that it was strictly a friends-with-benefits situation.

Just like I had told the girls, it would be with us.

I poured myself a glass of wine and got back to work. By the time nine o'clock rolled around, I had calculated nearly a million dollars' worth of funds that weren't accounted for.

Well, my job is done.

I typed up a basic email to Jorge, included an attachment of all of the discrepancies, and hit the "send" button. Whatever he decided to do with it was up to him. It was his business, after all, not mine. If Ria were my employee, then she would have been fired the second I noticed an inconsistency.

If Ria were my employee, she'd be sleeping with every man on my staff that was inclined to give in to her.

I shut off my laptop, slid into a satin nightgown, and then

hunkered down on the couch to watch television. But as much as I tried to tell myself not to worry about Jorge's business, the more worried I became. Sure, he had a history as a womanizer and mixed business with pleasure. But there was a good side to him too. He seemed to treat his employees incredibly well, and even though he was practically swimming in money, he often told me about all of the bonuses and perks he gave his employees.

Knowing that he was being taken advantage of made me feel a bit protective over him, and for a second, I thought about calling him.

No, Ginger. You have enough on your plate. Besides, he's a big boy and can take care of himself.

I just hoped that by taking care of himself, he'd get rid of Ria, because even though we were just friends-with-benefits, I couldn't stand the fact that she still worked for him.

The longer I tried to ignore the feeling in my stomach, the more I realized that I needed to speak with Jorge. I reached for my cell phone and called him. "Hey, it's Ginger. We need to talk."

6

Jorge

I told myself that one day I'd have a mansion as big as Chase and Margo's, but only when the time was right. Hopefully, it'd also be on Key Biscayne, not too far from theirs, so he and I could hang out all the time. Occasionally I thought about having one built for me right away, especially since there was some land available not too far from his property. But that type of investment didn't make much sense for a single guy like myself.

Besides, I loved my luxury penthouse with its private elevator. It'd cost me a pretty penny, but it was worth it. Sometimes I longed to have an actual house instead of a big apartment, though. It would be nice to have a yard or a home with its own private beach like Chase's. There was something so humbling about buying a place in the suburbs versus living in a penthouse. But until I was engaged or married—both of which seemed far into the future—it'd have to wait.

Although the more I looked at their home, the more I thought about having one built anyway. I could always rent it out until I was ready to move in. It'd only mean more money for me.

As I pulled into their long driveway, which had a massive water fountain in the middle, I admired its exquisite architecture. Chase had really pulled out all of the stops when he'd had it built. And to think that he had almost sold it because he'd been all alone, only to have Margo swoop in at the perfect time.

Their doorbell chimed so loudly that I was sure it could be heard from the street, which was several hundred feet away. Margo opened the door within seconds, with their one-year-old daughter, Joanna, clutching her arm.

"Jorge, come on in! I'm making fried chicken for dinner, so I hope you're hungry." She promptly handed me Joanna, who cooed as I held her and walked into the living room.

"Oh, man. I haven't had fried chicken in years. Bring it on!"

Chase took one look at me, holding his daughter and burst out laughing. "I cannot wait until you have kids, man. It'll be interesting to see how you do as a father."

I rolled my eyes while handing Joanna back to Margo, who slipped onto the back porch.

"Are you suggesting that I'd suck as a dad, Chase? Because

if memory serves me correctly, you weren't exactly father-material back in college."

It was our weekly hangout night, where we just sat in front of the television and drank beer. It was a way to catch up with each other since we were both so busy. We usually ordered a pizza, but I was more than happy to have some of Margo's fried chicken. That woman could cook up some of the best food in all of Florida.

"Whatever, man. All I'm saying is that one day, you're going to have a brood on your hands and be up to your ears in diapers."

I pictured myself with three or four kids, all screaming for my attention at once while I tried getting ready for work. *No, thank you.* "Yeah, me with kids. That'll be the day."

"It'll happen just when you least expect it," he said while handing me a beer from his armrest cooler. It was ice-cold too.

"How come Margo dipped? Does she not like me or something?"

Chase shot me a look while opening another beer for himself. "Why are you so paranoid all of a sudden? No, the waves are starting to pick up, and Joanna loves to watch them. I wouldn't be surprised if she turns into a water baby."

"What's a water baby?"

"You know when you can't get your kid out of the water."

"I thought every kid likes to play in the water."

"Nope," he said while changing the channel. "I hated the water growing up, but Ginger was a water baby. She used to spend hours in the ocean or pool, refusing to get out even when it was time to eat."

I nodded while sipping my beer, not wanting to discuss Ginger too much. Chase was very protective of his little sister, so much so that he had refused to give me her number last year. He had ended up giving her mine, which at the time felt like a slap in the face. Although everything seemed to be working out just fine.

"Well, hopefully, mine will be a water baby because I love swimming. I wish I had more leisure time lately, but all I ever do is work. Speaking of which, how's work going for you?"

He shrugged while landing on a home shopping channel, pitching some outdoor grill that seemed to get his attention. "Work is work. I've been thinking about getting into the pressure-cooker business, but I'm still doing research on how it works."

"I'm assuming that with your touch, it would be something you could control remotely."

"Of course," he said matter-of-factly. "What about your job? Anything new?"

"I officially broke things off with Ria."

Chase slammed his beer bottle down onto the coffee table before turning to face me. "Please tell me that you're serious this time, man."

"Hell, yes, I'm serious. Ria invited me out for drinks the night before I left for the States, and I made it abundantly clear that I'd text her to let her know if I could meet her."

"Let me guess: she went anyway and was pissed you didn't show up."

"Yup," I said while chugging the last of my beer. Chase promptly handed me another one. "Between the two of us, Ria and I haven't had sex in several months. We'd only been getting together to discuss work after-hours because I thought that maybe there'd be a spark between us, but there's nothing man. And when I look back on it, the sex was good but not great."

"Well, your next step should be to get rid of her as a business partner."

He was right, but Ria was so involved in my company that it would be a huge pain in the ass to get rid of her. I was hoping Ginger would find something so she'd just up and quit, then I could transfer the job responsibilities to someone already working for me.

"Speaking of which, I suspect that she's been embezzling money from me for quite some time."

Chase nearly dropped his bottle of beer that he'd just picked back up. "Why didn't you tell me sooner?"

"Because I knew you'd be on my ass about firing her, and it's not that simple. Do you know how many hours a day I work? And do you know how hard it is to find someone trustworthy to look into this sort of matter?"

As a billionaire, I attracted people who only wanted money. Which was why I had trusted Ria to look over my books. She had a successful, steady job, and her family was pretty well off too. If she were in desperate need of cash, she sure didn't act like it.

"I know it's difficult, but you could be losing millions of dollars, Jorge. You never should have had sex with her, man. The second you told me that you two hooked up, I knew it would be bad news."

"How could I forget that conversation we had months ago?"

I thought Chase would have been impressed that I'd slept with Ria, who could have easily passed as a supermodel with her hourglass figure and long, chestnut hair. Her face was perfect, with full, luscious lips, chiseled cheekbones, and eyelashes so long they tickled my forehead whenever we kissed.

But her soul was pure evil.

Chase had ripped into me that night, saying that I'd done the dumbest thing possible as a business owner. He reminded me that he was always surrounded by beautiful women he worked with and that you never mix business with pleasure.

"And what did I say to you that night, man?"

"That if I don't have the balls to turn down a woman's sexual advances, then I don't have the balls to be in business."

Ouch.

"Look, I said that to you because you're like my brother. Please tell me that you're having this looked into, and if you need someone to help you with it, I'm sure I could hook you up. Personally, that's not my thing, but—wait a minute. What about Ginger? That's basically what she does anyway, and you two talk all of the time!"

Yes, we talk all of the time and funny you should mention that because she is looking into it. Oh, and I had sex with your sister last night. And even though it didn't last that long, it was the best I've ever had. Is that cool, bro?

I froze in my seat, not knowing if I should tell Chase what had happened between Ginger and me the night before. Obviously skip over the details, since it was his sister, but tell him that it finally had happened.

Why should it matter to him? Both of us are grown adults, and it was consensual.

Our eyes met, and for a second, I thought he knew. Chase had always been highly intuitive.

Here we go.

But just as I went to tell him my cell phone rang—Ginger.

I held my finger up to Chase, who nodded, then I snuck onto the back porch. Margo ducked back into the house, giving me plenty of privacy to talk.

"Ginger, I was just thinking about you."

"I have good and bad news, Jorge. The good news is that I've finished going through your books, but the bad news is that there's a million dollars' worth of funds not accounted for."

My blood pressure skyrocketed as all of my suspicions were confirmed. "I knew it, Ginger! God, I am so stupid!"

"I know it's a little too late, but it's a terrible idea to mix business with pleasure. My guess is that Ria had you wrapped around her finger and knew that she could convince you not to look at the books. I'm so sorry."

I could hear the concern in Ginger's voice and truly believed her apology, even though she had nothing to do with my getting screwed over. "Well, I appreciate it, but this has nothing to do with you. I don't think that I can ever thank you enough, Ginger."

"Please, it's the least I could do since you gave me such a beautiful diamond tennis bracelet."

"That was a gift of congratulations for getting your degree, which is about to pay off with your new job. But I mean it, Ginger. I'm so lucky to have you in my life, and I don't know how I can ever repay you."

"Just promise me that you'll never hook up with any of your employees because this will get super messy."

Chase peeked his head out the back window at me, which was thankfully closed to keep the air conditioning inside.

Please don't come out here, man.

"I don't foresee that being an issue, Ginger. The hooking up with my employees, that is. Thankfully I have excellent lawyers, although I'm not sure which route I'll take." *Ask her out!* "Anyway, would you like to have dinner with me tomorrow night?" *Please say yes, please say yes!*

"I'd love to have dinner with you tomorrow night, Jorge."

"Perfect. I'll pick you up at seven o'clock."

As I hung up the phone, I slouched down onto a nearby chair and buried my face in my hands. I was filled with excitement at seeing Ginger again, and remorse at ever having gotten involved with Ria.

One. Million. Dollars.

Chase came out a few minutes later and sat down next to me. "What was that all about? One minute you're screaming into the phone, and the next, you're all excited. And now you look like death, no offense."

I leaned back in the chair and looked at Chase. "If Ria thinks that I've treated her like shit lately, then she's in for a rude awakening."

7

Ginger

It had been a busy day at Lavender Dreams Spa. We were lucky to rarely have anyone file any complaints, thanks in part to Guadalupe and Yuslan taking such good care of their clients, but when we did, it was usually messy. A woman claimed that she'd booked a two-hour massage online, even though the longest we offered was ninety minutes. After refusing to pay when the masseuse stopped at the scheduled time, she demanded a free treatment, or she'd leave us a bad review online.

Thankfully, Eva was a manager who could tell when a customer was lying. Much like Jorge could spot a fake diamond from a mile away...or so he had claimed.

Before taking my old position, she had gone to great lengths to familiarize herself with every service we provided. And that included understanding how our website worked. Even though most of our clients were good people, we still dealt with the occasional person who was looking for a free handout. And it was almost always the people who had the most money.

That seemed to be the case that morning too. Even the way the woman spoke suggested that paying for a luxury spa service was like water under the bridge. Which was odd, since she was looking for a free massage.

I couldn't help but eavesdrop as Eva showed her our website and asked where she clicked on the two-hour option.

The woman scoffed, saying it wasn't there anymore.

"And it's never been there, Mrs. Robinson. So while I'm very sorry for the misunderstanding, we will not be giving you a free treatment, and you do need to pay for services rendered today."

I giggled as it became quiet, followed by Mrs. Robinson pushing through the glass doors a few minutes later. I'd also heard her unzipping her purse, so clearly, the spa won. Several people started clapping as soon as the door shut, and when I finally poked my head out, I saw Eva hunched over the desk with her head in her hands.

"You handled that so well," I said while walking out to her.

One of the clients who was cashing out agreed with me. "Good for you. It's not right when customers pull that crap, and I'd bet good money that she knew exactly what she was doing."

We watched as Mrs. Robinson drove away from the spa in her expensive car, peeling out of the parking lot and nearly missing a construction worker who was trying to cross the street.

Eva and I made our way into the break room, where we poured ourselves a cup of coffee.

"At least you don't have a lot of those customers coming in here," I said while adding cream into my coffee.

"That's true, and I think that I handle them very well when it does happen. Aside from managing the schedules and some employee stuff, which comes with every job, it's pretty easy. To be honest, it feels too easy for me."

"What do you mean?"

Eva stared off into the distance as she spoke. "My life is so...simple, Ginger. All I do is work, hit the gym, watch a movie, and repeat the cycle. I miss having a boyfriend." Eva was definitely the relationship-type who didn't do well on her own; I'd come to realize that some people were simply wired that way.

Thankfully I'm not like that...anymore.

"Well, enjoy it now because it won't be long until a guy snatches you up. And remember that relationships aren't always fun. When I look back at some of mine, I realize they were more stressful than enjoyable."

"That's true, and I'm starting not to miss Anthony anymore. How are things with you and Jorge, by the way?"

Somehow I found a way to hide my excitement. "Great.

We're having dinner tonight." Eva's right eyebrow went into a hook, as usual. "As friends, Eva. Just as friends."

After work, I went straight home to get ready for dinner. My stomach was grumbling loudly, but I fought the urge to eat something ahead of time.

As I took a quick shower, I started thinking about Ria again. It was only a matter of time before Jorge had to deal with her, and based on everything he'd said to me, she sounded like a woman who always got her way. I hadn't seen what she looked like, though. Ria either had her social media accounts set to private, or she avoided it altogether.

But knowing Jorge, she was probably drop-dead gorgeous.

The good news, I told myself, was that Jorge was suspicious enough of her to have me look over the books. And she really was embezzling money. Anyone who'd just graduated with their accounting degree or was still in college could have figured that out. But what would happen when he confronted her? Would he have the balls to fire her ass and take her to court, or would she seduce him back into bed?

Stop thinking that way, Ginger. He's just a friend.

I chose a hot-pink dress and black high heels and spent a little too much time applying makeup. I found myself getting angry as I tried to cake on the mascara, only to wipe it all off and start over again.

This is silly. Of course, Jorge isn't going to go back to Ria! What kind of man would sleep with a woman who's stolen nearly a million dollars out from underneath him?

A man who avoided relationships and had the money to

still take her to court, right after they were done sleeping with each other. Let's face it: even if Ria showed proof of their physical relationship, Jorge could afford the best attorney to still throw Ria under the bus. And what man wouldn't want one last romp in the sack with a woman who, from what it sounded like, was as sexy as her?

I spritzed on some rose-scented perfume, tousled my hair a little bit, and then waited for Jorge to show up. It was six o'clock, and he wasn't due to come over until seven.

Realizing there was no way to think about anything other than Ria and Jorge's relationship, I opened up my laptop and started reviewing the documents again. Ria had a seven-figure salary, so what did she need all of the extra money for? She was literally his business partner, and both of them could quit tomorrow and never have to worry about money again.

Just as I was about to do some research, my doorbell rang. It scared me so bad that I jumped up, causing my laptop to tumble onto the floor. Thankfully my floor was carpeted, though.

Get it together, Ginger.

I opened the door to see Jorge standing there, holding a bouquet of green hydrangeas.

Why do you have to be so alto, oscuro y guapo?

"Oh, wow, Jorge! They're beautiful. Thank you."

After putting them in a vase full of water, we got into his car and drove off to a local Italian restaurant. The hostess sat us at a private, half-circle, red-velvet booth in a dining room I didn't even know existed.

Just as she was about to flirt with Jorge, since I'd stopped along the way to fix my shoe strap, she saw me sliding into the other side of the booth. "Enjoy your meal."

Jorge winked at me once I got situated into the booth. "How was work today?"

"It was all right, although Eva had to deal with a customer trying to get a free service."

"That's pretty messed up, but it doesn't surprise me. The world is full of people trying to get something for nothing."

I wanted to keep that part of the conversation going, hoping he'd mention Ria and his plans, but he fell silent while looking over the menu.

"That's true. Thankfully Eva put her in her place while keeping it professional. She's so good at it too. I would have crumbled if that'd happened to me, but that girl knows how to deal with people."

After placing our orders, Jorge and I spent the evening discussing our careers. He went into great detail about what it took to be a diamond broker and that it wasn't all about shiny bracelets and massive rings. I, on the other hand, told him about what I did all day at the spa.

"The spa is lucky to have someone as loyal as you are, Ginger."

"I really am loyal, almost to a fault. I've been working for Guadalupe and Yuslan for several years now, and I can't see going anywhere else. It's a perfect job. You should get a facial sometime."

"Are you suggesting that my skin is bad?"

"Oh, God, no! In fact, you have magnificent skin. I just know that a lot of guys think facials are just for women, but we have just as many males as we do female clients who regularly get them done."

Jorge was doubled over with laughter as I explained what I meant. "I was just kidding, Ginger. I get them all the time back in Belgium, so maybe I'll book an appointment this week." He took my hand and slowly rubbed it from across the table. "I'm just dreading having to deal with everything at work, if you know what I mean."

"I can only imagine what's going through your mind, but at least you know."

We sat in silence for a few moments, the only noise coming from the low talking of fellow diners, and I was waiting for him to tell me that he'd be firing her.

Instead, he pulled out the dessert menu and started looking it over. "I'm in the mood for some tiramisu. What about you?"

After dinner, he invited me back to his penthouse. Even though I had no intention of having sex with him again, I accepted since I could just walk home afterward. We rode up in his private elevator, which was plated with gold.

Jorge's penthouse had floor-to-ceiling windows that gave him a breathtaking view of Miami. His furniture had been custom-made, and he even had a piano in his living room. Even though we'd been friends for a year and lived next door to each other, the other night was the only time I'd been in his home. I had missed the details between his office and his getting me naked in his bedroom. So I took the opportunity to walk around in awe of just how glamorous Jorge's space was, as he poured each of us a glass of red wine.

"I'm actually somewhat of a minimalist, although you may not be able to tell. I just needed the stuff to fill up all of this space."

"Yeah, I wouldn't call this a minimalist penthouse. Good for you, though. With all of the long hours you work and everything you put up with, you deserve a place like this."

He pressed something on his phone and music started playing throughout the entire space. Jorge took my hand, and we started dancing, waltzing across the room just as we had done at my party. I allowed myself to rest my head against his shoulder, even though my intuition was telling me to pull away and go home.

Thank him for a beautiful evening and say that you have an early day tomorrow.

But I couldn't.

The longer we danced, the harder I pressed my body against his. He was so tall, dark, and handsome, and any other woman in my position would have done the same thing. Hell, practically every woman he ever flirted with *had* done the exact same thing.

Ria.

I lifted my head, and our eyes met. But instead of pulling away, I let him lead me toward his bedroom, where we continued dancing to the romantic jazz playing throughout the penthouse. Every sway of his hips pulled me closer to him, and by the time the song transitioned into another one, I had lost all control of my senses.

"Jorge," I whispered as our lips were merely inches away from each other.

"Yes?"

"I…"

And that was it. I leaned in to kiss Jorge, and as our mouths met, I fell backward onto his bed with him on top of me.

8

Jorge

Ginger's body felt even more delicate than the last time we had made love. As I practically ripped off her hot-pink dress, all I could think about was how I'd told myself this wouldn't happen again. Ginger simply wasn't the friends-with-benefits type of woman, nor should she be. A woman of her caliber deserved to be wined, dined, and treated like a queen. But as she lay there on my bed wearing only her black high heels, all I could think about was being deep inside of her again.

My clothes carelessly fell to the floor as I slid out of them, refusing to let my eyes drift away from Ginger's magnificent body. She leaned against the pillows, resting her head on top of them as I positioned my cock up against her pussy.

"Ginger," I groaned before kissing her.

She let out a deep moan as I slid my shaft into her warm womanhood, before proceeding to wrap her legs around my waist. The only sounds in the room were of the bed creaking, her heels clacking together, and our lustful sighs of pleasure. I leaned back on my knees, grabbed her hips, and pulled her farther against my cock with every thrust of my body.

"God, yes, Jorge! Harder!"

I flipped her onto all fours, then started pounding her from behind. She didn't seem like the type of woman to leave high heels on during sex, but that was what I was beginning to love. It was like getting a little surprise once you got back to the bedroom.

Ginger arched her back as she let out a massive moan, screaming so loud as she squirted all over my cock. Her juices drenched my dick as I slammed harder into her, my heavy, aching balls hitting her clit as I pounded away. I reached my arm around and rubbed her sensitive nub, which was growing in size by the minute. I had every intention of finishing that way too.

But Ginger had other plans.

She leaned backward, causing me to fall onto my torso as she rode me reverse cowgirl. Her gorgeous, plump ass cheeks bounced up and down as I stayed inside of her, grinding her wetness all over my pulsating cock. Then she pushed all the way back until our heads were right next to each other.

We looked into each other's eyes as I kept pounding her, never pulling away as both of us climaxed at the same time.

Her legs started shaking as my balls emptied into her core, and her screams of pleasure almost kept me hard for a second round. Unfortunately, my grueling work schedule had left me winded.

Ginger regretfully slid off of me, and we laid next to each other for a few moments. "Jorge, I...didn't expect that to happen."

I took her hand in mine and began rubbing her palm with my thumb. "Neither did I, Ginger. Neither did I."

I woke up the next morning to Ginger sleeping on my chest, which felt so good that I didn't want to move. And while I couldn't predict what would become of our relationship, one thing was for sure—Ria had to go.

Sliding carefully out of bed so as not to wake her up, I tiptoed into the kitchen and started a pot of coffee. Ria often acted as though she had balls bigger than mine, but that morning I would be putting her in place. I prepared my speech to her repeatedly in my head while the coffee brewed, and after guzzling a cup, I gave her a call.

Here goes nothing.

"Good morning, dear. How's everything going in the States?"

"Cut the bullshit, Ria. I know you've been embezzling money out of the company."

There was an incredibly long pause on her end, which was odd since Ria had never been shy with her words. "Jorge, it's not what you think. If you hadn't flown back to Miami without telling me, perhaps we could have discussed this over dinner. I know how much you love my lasagna."

Your lasagna tastes like rubber covered in cheap ketchup.

"There's nothing to explain, Ria. You've stolen nearly a million dollars out from underneath me, and for what? Is your seven-figure salary not enough for you? Did you not inherit enough money from your father's estate?"

"I knew this would happen, Jorge. Say no more. I'm hopping on the next flight to Miami so we can straighten out this whole ordeal."

The sound of Ginger moving around in bed caught my attention until I peeked in and saw that she'd just switched positions.

"There's no reason for you to come to Miami, Ria. Just know that you and I are done, both personally and professionally!"

"Screw you, Jorge Stein! None of this would be happening if we were married, and you know why? Because all of the accounts would be jointly owned!"

"Have you lost your damn mind? You actually think that I'd want to marry you? Look, I've moved on, and you need to as well. I'm going to buy you out of your partnership." The sound of Ria zipping up a suitcase was all I could hear for a few minutes. "Were you planning on coming here anyway?"

"Of course, darling. You didn't think you'd get rid of me that quickly, did you? I've spent the best years of my life waiting on a proposal, and I intend to get one."

"You are insane, Ria! I'm buying you out of your partnership, not asking you to be my wife, and that's final. Or else I'll go straight to my lawyers."

"You're not buying me out of anything, and do you realize how long and drawn out that process would be? And remember that I have just as much leverage in the diamond industry as you, if not more."

Beads of sweat formed on my forehead as I realized she was right. Of course, she was right. That was probably why she knew she could steal so much money from me too.

"What are you suggesting, Ria?"

She chuckled into the phone. "You know damn well what I'm suggesting, Jorge. I can make it so that no diamond-mine union wants anything to do with you. Maybe I'll start my own company and offer them three times what you're paying them right now, or maybe I'll steal all of your employees out from underneath you."

Ria needed to be out of my life as soon as possible.

"It'll only be a waste of your time and money, Ria, because I'm in love with another woman." I heard her gasp, and only wish I'd seen her look of horror in person.

"You are not, Jorge! You've never loved any woman besides me."

"For the record, I've never loved you. And not only am I in love, but we're getting married next week!"

Ria started tapping her long nails against a hard surface. "I don't believe you, Jorge. You're not a guy who will ever get married. Don't you know that by now? You're a lifelong bachelor who can't commit to anyone! And with me, you could have had it all. I would have married you and looked the other way when you fooled around with other women. Better yet, I might have even joined you."

A year ago, those last words would have given me a massive erection. But all I wanted to do was vomit. I wanted to tell her that I never even enjoyed our sex that much to begin with, and it was only out of convenience that we'd slept together.

"You don't believe me, huh? Then why am I having a small, private wedding ceremony next week, Ria? Because I'm in love, and it sure as hell isn't with you!" Once again, she went silent, but I knew she wasn't crying. Ria didn't have it in her to cry over a man. "I swear to God, Ria, don't you dare get on that plane and come to Miami. You and I couldn't be more over, do you hear me? And I don't know how, but I'll be getting all of the money you embezzled back! Perhaps you've forgotten that I have the best lawyers in all of Miami!"

Ria hung up, and just as I was about to throw my phone into the living room, Ginger walked into the kitchen.

"Is everything all right? I thought I was dreaming that you were yelling, but I guess it wasn't a dream."

I quietly set down the phone and poured her a cup of coffee. Ginger sat across from me, holding her head up with one hand. She was exhausted.

"Well, I'm sorry it woke you up, but I called Ria out on her lies. I told her that I know she's stolen nearly a million dollars from the company."

Ginger's head shot up. "How did she take it?"

"Not well, but that's to be expected. I'm sure Ria didn't think I'd find out about the missing money, especially since we had a thing going on."

Ginger nodded while sipping her coffee. "It's good that you confronted her, Jorge. You don't need someone like that working for you. Or, in your case, with you. She was your partner."

My body tensed as I realized the predicament I had just gotten myself into. When Ria shows up and sees that I'm not getting married, it'll be harder to get rid of her.

"I offered to buy her out of her partnership, but—"

"What? Why aren't you letting your lawyers handle this? That's what you pay them for!"

I leaned back in my chair while nodding. "Ria is very conniving, Ginger. The longer she's in my life, the more she'll make it a complete hell. If I gave this to my lawyers, we'd be tied up for months or years with a court case. This way, I can just get rid of her."

Ginger seemed to understand my point but was apprehensive. "Yeah, but just be careful and document everything. I'm no lawyer, but...anyway, do what you gotta do." After finishing her coffee, we kissed, and she went back home to get ready for work.

But before I started work myself, I picked my phone back up and called Chase.

"Dude, why are you up so early?"

"I told Ria that I know she's been embezzling money, Chase, and it did not go well." I overheard Margo ask who was on the phone before Chase's feet made their way downstairs.

"Of course it didn't because she's crazy. So, what's going to happen now?"

"Well, I offered to just pay her to leave the company because getting my lawyers involved would only drag this out. Plus, she has so many connections in the diamond industry that she could royally screw me over."

I heard him pouring water into his coffee machine. "That's a good point, although it'd be easier on you if the lawyers handled it."

"Anyway, she started telling me that none of this would be an issue if we were married."

"What the hell difference would that make?"

"Because we'd have joint bank accounts, and I could track the money myself."

Chase let out a long whistle. "God, Jorge. You really dodged a bullet with this one."

"Not exactly. Ria threatened to fly to Miami as soon as I called her out. I told her that I was in love with another woman and that I'd moved on."

"Ha, way to lie. Like you could ever be in love with a woman."

Don't be so sure about that, Chase.

"When she didn't believe me, I told her that I was engaged and getting married next week. But she didn't believe it, and now she's flying out here! What the hell am I going to do? I can't exactly avoid this woman, either. She knows where I live and work."

I listened to Chase pull out a chair and sit down. "Leave it to you to get wrapped up in something this insane, Jorge."

"I'm serious! I'm freaking out right now! When Ria sees that I'm obviously not getting married, she'll refuse my offer to buy her out of her partnership, and then I'll be tied up with legal crap for who knows how long. Oh, God!"

"What?"

"The De Veers Diamond Group. She's still in charge of negotiations with the unions and will use that as leverage against me. When she sees that I'm not engaged, the second I hire lawyers, she'll be all over that and really screw me over! What am I going to do, Chase?"

"So, you're saying that unless Ria actually sees you getting married, that she'll find a way to basically force you into bankruptcy?"

Sweat was now forming on my forehead. "Yes. Please, Chase. You're a smart man and one of my best friends. What do I do?"

"Two words, Jorge—fake bride."

9

Ginger
Two Days Later

We had a staff meeting at work that day, and if I hadn't set my alarm clock, I would have been late. Not that Guadalupe would have minded, of course. She would have suspected that it had something to do with Jorge and demanded to know all of the details, which would entail worrying my ass off about him sleeping with Ria again. As much as I tried focusing on what Guadalupe was talking about, my mind kept going back to Jorge's phone conversation the previous day.

I was up all night, tossing and turning as I wondered how Jorge would ultimately end things with Ria. I kept picturing him picking her up at the airport, taking her back to his penthouse, and having sex with her.

But every time I woke up, I reminded myself of what I'd overheard Jorge telling Ria on the phone the day before: he was in love with someone else. Unless I had been dreaming that part.

Of course, you were because Jorge is a womanizer.

After Jorge and I had made love the other night, I passed out and dreamed about him. The two of us were having a picnic in a park, feeding each other strawberries while Chase and Margo were there with Joanna. We didn't talk too much, and what few words we did say I couldn't remember. But I did remember feeling as though I were in love with him.

I focused my attention back on Guadalupe, who discussed some new types of facials the spa would be offering. Not that any of it affected my job, since I did all of the accounting. But it was good to know for when I scheduled a treatment for myself.

After the meeting, I went back to my office and resumed work as usual. My fingers started hitting the keys a bit harder than necessary, and I realized that it was purely out of jealousy. I was jealous that Jorge had spoken with Ria the other morning, even though I—and probably all of the neighbors—could tell that he was ending things with her. Even when he said to me that it was over, while we drank our coffee, I could tell he was serious. He would do just about anything to altogether remove Ria from his life.

But he also seemed a bit distant, as though he were hiding

something. Would Ria require one more romp in the sack before leaving the company?

Stop being so paranoid. You're just two friends who sleep together.

Except I had never been that type of woman, nor did I think I had it in me to become one. How much longer could I keep having sex with Jorge without a firm commitment?

While I was typing away on my keyboard, Margo poked her head into my office.

"If you pound on those keys any harder, the paintings on the wall will fall off."

I motioned for her to come inside my office and sit down. "What brings you in today?"

"I was in desperate need of a facial, and I just overheard Yuslan talking about their new ones. They sound even better than what I just had done. Why do you seem so tense, though?"

I powered off my monitor and shut the door. "All right, this has to stay between us. You know how Jorge has had an ongoing relationship with Ria?"

"Oh, yeah. Jorge was at our place when you called him the other night. Did you look into that whole embezzlement issue for him?"

"Yup."

"Now I know why he called Chase so early yesterday morning. I meant to ask him about it before I left for my appointment, but he had a conference call."

"Anyway, Ria has embezzled nearly a million dollars from

Jorge's business. He's suspected it for quite some time, but because they were having sex didn't push the issue."

Margo's mouth fell wide open as she gasped. "A million dollars? That's insane! Granted, a million isn't much money for Jorge, but that's not exactly chump change. Thank God you caught it for him."

"I was hoping he'd get his lawyers involved, but apparently he just wants to buy her out of her partnership with him."

Margo picked up on how tense I was, despite my best efforts to conceal it. "Well, I wouldn't get too upset about it, Ginger. You did him a favor, and he'll probably come to his senses and have his lawyers take care of it. I'm not sure why he wouldn't automatically go that route."

"Because he's worried that it'll take too long, and with all of her connections in the diamond business, she can really screw him over. I told him to just hand it over to his lawyers, but he just had to call Ria yesterday morning!"

Calm down, woman!

"Ginger, why are you getting so upset? She didn't embezzle money from you."

I nodded while staring at my desk, not wanting to admit my real reason for being so angry. "I just hate seeing my friends being taken advantage of like that."

Margo folded her arms while leaning back in the chair. "Did you spend the night at Jorge's the other night?"

I couldn't bring myself to look into her eyes.

"I knew you two would get together again! So, that's why

you're so upset. You're worried about something happening between him and Ria."

I finally looked up at her and nodded. "And why wouldn't it, Margo? They had the same type of situation that we do: friends-with-benefits. And Jorge has never been in a serious, long-term relationship. I played right into his hands, didn't I?"

Margo shook her head while leaning across the desk, her long, gold necklace hitting its surface. "Ginger, people change over time. I don't think you should jump to any conclusions regarding Jorge and Ria, especially since he seems so into you." She held up my wrist, pointing to the diamond tennis bracelet. "Do you think he would have gotten that for you if he didn't have feelings?"

"Really, Margo? He's a diamond broker. Of course, he'd get that for me regardless of his feelings. It's an instant pass into my panties." She let out a sigh while leaning back in her chair. "All of this is my fault too. I never should have slept with him, Margo. Look at this beautiful office that Guadalupe gave me! This is my dream job, and all I can think about is some woman in Belgium sleeping with Jorge."

"Try not to think about it too much, Ginger. Something tells me that Jorge is going to change his ways because even Chase says that he seems to be maturing. Just give it some time. Maybe you should try working from home for a while too. I'm sure Guadalupe wouldn't mind."

"That would only put me closer to Jorge, and right now, I think I need some space. Although, he's probably at the office today."

Margo's cell phone went off with a text message. "Oh, shoot. Chase has a conference call, and Joanna won't stop crying. I gotta go. Call me later, all right?"

As soon as Margo left, I sent Guadalupe an email asking if I could work from home for the rest of the afternoon due to a headache. She replied within seconds, telling me to take the rest of the day off, and to just rest.

God, I love her.

It would do me well to relax on the couch, order some pizza, and clear my mind.

I pulled into my reserved parking spot back at home, eager to get out of work clothes and into some shorts. As soon as I shut the car door, I turned to look toward Jorge's penthouse. It had become a habit of mine ever since he had returned to Miami.

He wasn't home.

Phew.

And just as I was about to walk inside, I saw his convertible pull into the parking lot.

Jorge had a woman next to him.

I quickly ducked behind my car until only my eyes were peering over it. They got out and headed into his building, and my jaw dropped as soon as I saw the woman. She wasn't just beautiful. She was drop-dead gorgeous, and I had no doubt that it was Ria.

Once they were inside, I ran into my condo, slammed the door shut, and immediately called Eva.

"Hey, did you leave work early? I stopped by your office

with some pastries that Guadalupe made, but it was locked, and your car wasn't in the parking lot."

"Jorge is having sex with Ria right this very second, Eva!"

"What? Wait, let me shut my office door. Calm down and tell me everything, Ginger."

I paced back and forth in my living room, trying to calm my nerves when all I wanted to do was bang on his door. "He just got out of his car with this tall woman who looked straight out of a fashion magazine, or one of those social media influencers, and both of them went into his penthouse! I knew he would sleep with her again, Eva!"

"Relax, Ginger. I'm sure there's a logical explanation for why she's at his place."

I sat down on my couch, unable to control my legs from shaking. "No, you don't understand, Eva. Jorge suspected Ria of embezzling from him, so he asked me to look over his books. Which, of course, I did, because everyone just loves to use me!"

"Ginger—"

"And I told him she had stolen almost a million dollars! But did he go to his lawyers? Of course not! He's planning on buying her out, but that conniving woman is having sex with him right now! I just know it, Eva! He can't stay away from her!"

I broke down sobbing on my couch, with nothing but images of them having sex running through my mind.

"Ginger, as someone who has been cheated on very

recently, I guarantee that's not what's happening. He's probably just going over things with her in person."

I dried my eyes with a tissue, which only caused my mascara to smudge all over my face. "If Jorge wanted to go over things with Ria in person, he would have gone to a coffeehouse, a restaurant, or his office in downtown Miami. He wouldn't have brought Ria back to his penthouse in the middle of the afternoon when he knew that I'd be at work!"

All I could do was sob uncontrollably as Eva listened, not knowing what to say to calm me down. And how could I blame her? The only thing that could have calmed me down was a logical explanation for Ria being at Jorge's penthouse.

"Ginger, I'm so sorry. What can I do?"

I looked in the mirror while drying my eyes, not even bothering to clean up the mascara that was all over the place. "You can thank your lucky stars that you're single, Eva, because men are nothing but trouble!"

10

Jorge

Miami International Airport was packed as usual, which meant there was too much of a risk of me being seen with Ria. But what other choice did I have? Her plane was due any minute, and if I hadn't agreed to pick her up, then I could only imagine what she would have done. Knowing her, she would have figured out that I'd been sleeping with Ginger and approached her at Lavender Dreams Spa.

I winced while thinking about what a scene that would have been. Ria was a ruthless woman without a soul, although she'd make one hell of a private investigator.

I paced back and forth in front of my convertible, impatiently waiting for her to show up. She'd demanded that we discuss everything at my place, and I would have refused if it'd been later on that evening when Ginger would be home from work. The last thing I wanted was for her to even get one look at Ria. The sooner Ria was out of my life, the sooner I could focus on my relationship with Ginger.

I glared at the hands ticking on my gold Rolex. "Come on, Ria. I don't have all day."

I knew that Chase was right about having to pull off a fake wedding too. If I couldn't convince Ria that afternoon to accept my final offer, what other choice did I have? I'd have to introduce her to a woman, say she was my fiancée, and then hopefully she'd buy it. But knowing Ria, that wouldn't be enough. She'd probably insist on attending the damn wedding.

I looked up as an Air Antwerp flight prepared to land, and suddenly I felt like puking. The mere thought of having to look at Ria's face made me want to hurl all over the pavement.

She emerged shortly from the airport, dressed to impress in some designer leopard mini-skirt and a white halter top that barely contained her obnoxiously large, fake breasts. Her oversized sunglasses nearly touched the top of her crimson lips. Any other man would have instantly fawned over her, but I backed away from her outstretched arms.

"Just get in the car, Ria."

She snapped her fingers at the poor airline attendant who was rolling around her luggage. I helped as he struggled to fit everything inside my trunk.

"Are you moving to Miami or something? What's with all of the bags?"

Ria didn't say a word as she insisted the airline associate open the door for her.

I held up my hand, gave him a one-hundred-dollar bill, and shook my head. "That won't be necessary. Ria can open her own damn door."

Her eyes were hidden behind her obnoxious glasses, but it was clear that I'd offended her.

God, that felt good.

The first several minutes of our car ride was spent in silence. If it had been the same situation several months before, the sexual tension would have been too much for us to handle. I would have pulled the car over somewhere and had my hands all over her. But instead of being aroused by Ria, I had the complete opposite of an erection —shrinkage.

"So, Jorge. What's your fiancée's name? Or should I assume it's Ginger?"

"Don't worry about that, Ria. Where are you staying while in town?"

Because it sure as hell ain't with me.

"Where else would I stay, darling? At your penthouse, of course."

I nearly slammed on the brakes on 42nd Avenue. "That's not even an option, Ria. I don't care if you sleep outside on the street, but there's no way that you're staying with me."

"Relax," she said as we got onto the highway. "I have my own place in Miami Beach now, remember?"

"Vaguely. But why don't we kill some time, since it looks

like traffic is pretty bad today? Explain the missing money, Ria."

She let out a long sigh while pretending to enjoy the beautiful views of the ocean. "Oh, Jorge. I have all of the paperwork right here in my purse. Everything is accounted for, all right? Let's have this discussion at your place."

"The only reason I'm even letting you into my home is that I don't want to be seen with you in public. And I mean it. I want you out of this partnership, once and for all. Whatever is on that paperwork is probably complete garbage, anyway."

"It's not like I haven't been to your penthouse before, Jorge. I remember it like the back of my hand. In fact, I can still feel your large bed underneath me as you—"

"Stop it, Ria! Now."

If I hadn't been so concerned about her ruining my reputation within the diamond community, I would have gotten a court order against her and handed everything over to my lawyers. I couldn't believe that I'd ever gotten mixed up with her in the first place. Sure, she had been pretty good in bed and knew how to do her part in the business aspect. But her beauty was only skin deep.

And after being with Ginger, I realized that Ria wasn't all that pretty in the first place. She'd gotten far too much plastic surgery on her face, slowly morphing into a creepy doll that looked like a cat, and her fake breasts were too damn hard. The first time I had pressed my body up against them, I had winced in disgust.

She was the complete opposite of Ginger; whose soft and feminine body was perfect in every way.

As we pulled into the parking lot of my penthouse, I was thankful that Ginger was at work that afternoon. She had made it clear that while Guadalupe had given her the option to work from home, she didn't use it because she loved working at the spa. She and Eva got to gossip on their breaks, and I was sure she was looking forward to when Margo returned from maternity leave.

I threw the car into park and rushed inside, vaguely hearing Ria ask why I wasn't helping her with her luggage. "Because you're not staying here, Ria. Now get inside so we can get this over with."

The two of us sat down at my dining room table, which was large enough to seat a dozen people. Ria tried sitting down next to me, but I pointed to the opposite end to keep her far away. She practically threw a bunch of paperwork in front of me, which I quickly scanned as she tapped her fingers on the table.

"You don't have to read every damn line, Jorge."

"Bullshit."

It took me about fifteen minutes to review everything, and my blood was boiling by the time I was done. I sat back in the chair and glared at Ria.

"Why are you so angry, Jorge? I told you it was no big deal. I would never steal from you!"

"You're really something else, aren't you, Ria? Did you

think I'd buy any of this crap? Everything you have listed here is a bogus expense!"

Ria let out a huff while looking away, pretending to admire my million-dollar artwork on the walls. "If you're short on cash, Jorge, just tell me, and I'll spot you some. There's no reason for you to go through this just to get some money."

I threw the papers in her direction, causing them to scatter all over my marble table. "You know damn well that I can spot a fake diamond from a mile away, Ria! What makes you think it's not the same with these so-called legal documents?"

Ria stood up and made her way over to me, very slowly while sashaying her hips. "You know what you need, Jorge? You need to relax. And if memory serves me correctly, I know just what to do."

I stood up as she was about to get onto her knees. "Stop it, Ria, right now! I mean it. It's over between us! And I'm sorry if I've misled you, really I am."

Ria's hands turned into fists at her sides. "You son of a bitch, Jorge! You *have* been leading me on all of this time! If you didn't like me so much, then why have we been sleeping together? Why did we have sex nearly every damn night while you were in Antwerp?"

"We haven't been intimate in months, Ria."

She started walking toward me. "That's because of Ginger. You say she's just a friend, but I know she's the reason for all of this Jorge. I bet you wasted no time getting your dick wet with her too!"

I put up my hand to stop her from getting any closer. As much as I enjoyed venting my frustrations at her, we needed to keep it about business. "You need to calm down, Ria, because regardless of how we feel toward each other, the truth is that we're still legally connected. Now sit back down at the table so we can get through everything, all right?"

Ria yanked out a chair and sat down, once again drumming her nails. "So, what now?"

"Once again, I'm offering you a large sum of money to buy out your partnership. Five-hundred million dollars. Considering that you embezzled nearly a million dollars, I'd say that's a pretty good deal, Ria."

She rolled her eyes at me. "Oh, please. Do you really think I'd accept a measly half-billion dollars out of you, Jorge? You're worth so much more than that, honey, and you know that I can ruin your career in an instant. I have more leverage in the diamond industry than you think, possibly even more than you."

"Bullshit, Ria! What more do you want out of me? I can't think of anyone else who would turn down all of this money, given that you could be jailed for theft! Which would you rather do? Spend your life behind bars, or walk away with a shitload of money? Your choice."

All I could think about was Ginger, and how much better my life would be once I was with her and not Ria. Ginger didn't care about this sort of stuff. Sure, she liked diamonds and probably the fact that I made a lot of money. But she wasn't anywhere near as superficial as Ria, and she was beginning to bring out the best in me.

"The longer I'm in business with you, Jorge, the more money I make. So, long story short: I'm not going anywhere. And you know what I want out of you."

I leaned back in my chair, pretending to play dumb. "Do tell, Ria."

"I want marriage, Jorge. Let's face it. I'm getting older by the day. Sure, you say that you're in love with another woman, but you know how perfect we are together. And it's not just the sex, Jorge. We're in the same industry, for God's sake! That should be enough of a reason for you to marry me!"

I stood up and started pacing, right in front of the large window that overlooked the Atlantic Ocean. "What will it take, Ria, for you to understand that I don't want to marry you? Better yet, let me be abundantly clear. The only reason we ever slept together was that it was convenient for both of us, and we needed each other professionally."

"Your mouth says you don't want me, Jorge, but the one between your legs says otherwise."

"It might have at one time, Ria, but that's in the past."

Tears formed in her eyes as she grabbed her purse and marched toward the front door, her heels clicking against the marble floor. But before she left, she whipped her head back around to look at me. "You haven't seen the last of me, Jorge. And you can stop lying about being engaged because you know damn well that I'm the best you've ever had!"

11

Ginger
One Week Later

It was pretty crowded that night at the restaurant. Eva and I were sitting at the bar, each of us nursing a pina colada while discussing work gossip. She had overheard one of the new hairstylists confessing to an affair with her gardener, and her excuse was that her husband was sleeping with one of their neighbors. Usually, I'd be excited to hear all of the details, but the last thing I wanted to think about was sex.

All I could think about was Jorge getting back together with Ria.

Part of me regretted not going over to his penthouse that day when Ria was inside with him, but I didn't know how I'd react. Legally he could do whatever he wanted, and if I showed up, I would have only made things worse. But that didn't stop me from thinking about what could have happened, though. I pictured walking in on them having sex, screaming at them as they saw me, and then storming off. Really drive it home to Jorge that he'd screwed up and would never get me back.

He had been texting me every day for the past week, ever since I saw him come home with her in the passenger seat. Not a day went by where he didn't beg for me to tell him what he had done wrong, nor did I feel compelled to call him out on his lies. The two times we'd slept together only confirmed that he was a womanizer I never should have gotten involved with. And even though I was still wearing his diamond tennis bracelet, I finally saw it for what it was—a passport into my panties.

Which was precisely what I'd told Margo.

"Ginger? Are you listening to anything that I'm saying?" Eva made me realize that I was staring off into the distance.

"I'm so sorry, Eva. You were saying that her husband travels a lot or something?"

She shook her head at me while looking concerned. "You're thinking about Jorge again, aren't you?"

I glanced down at my phone, secretly hoping that he had texted or called me again. But there was nothing. In fact, it had been several hours since he last made any attempt to contact me. "I can't worry about him anymore, Eva. Because the more I do, the more I find it impossible to focus on work.

And I didn't spend all of that time in college to throw away a career over some guy."

"I know you're worried about ruining your new career, Ginger, but I've never seen you this depressed before."

Eva wasn't wrong.

"If he and I hadn't formed such a strong bond before it happened, then I'd probably be over him by now. But we were friends for a whole year, and then he goes and sleeps with Ria after he had told me it was over between them! After I spent my time looking over his books for him! Do you realize what a slap in the face that is, Eva?"

She nodded while sipping the rest of her drink.

Just thinking about it made me want to burst out crying, right there in the middle of the bar. I had never felt more screwed over than I had with Jorge, and it was so hard to think about anything other than him sleeping with her.

"But how do you know they slept together, Ginger?"

I dabbed at the few tears streaming down my cheeks with a tissue. "Oh, come on, Eva. She came home with him in the middle of the afternoon on a workday. Who does that sort of thing?"

"But wasn't he trying to buy her out of her partnership in the business? Maybe that's why she was back at his place."

I shook my head defiantly while trying to suppress the tears streaming down my face, which might as well have been Niagara Falls. "No, Eva. Jorge would have done that somewhere public, not in his own damn penthouse. Oh, God! I can't believe this is happening. I can't even go a day without crying over some guy! Who am I anymore? This isn't me, Eva! I don't want to be so hung up over a damn guy!"

I accidentally knocked my purse onto the ground. As I picked it back up, Chase and Jorge walked into the restaurant. Jorge and I locked eyes for several seconds, and my heart started beating too fast. I could hear Guadalupe's voice saying, "What an alto, oscuro y guapo man!"

And he was.

Even though I was filled with rage over what he'd done, I also couldn't deny that over the year of us talking on the phone, I had learned he was everything I'd ever wanted in a man.

I threw two twenty-dollar bills onto the bar and ran out the door.

Jorge grabbed my hand as soon as I stepped outside, though. "Ginger, please don't leave! Why aren't you returning my calls or text messages?"

I turned to face him, and his mouth fell open when he saw how upset I was. "Oh, please, Jorge! I knew you'd go back to Ria! You just couldn't wait to get her back into bed, could you?"

Jorge looked genuinely confused as he tilted his head at me. "What the hell are you talking about?"

"I should have known better. What hurts the most is the fact that we built a friendship before it all happened. Every week we'd talk on the phone, and I'd always go to bed with the biggest smile on my face. Even though I told myself we were just friends, deep down, of course, I was falling for you!"

"Ginger, I haven't slept with Ria in months!"

I yanked my hand away from him but stopped myself from leaving. If our relationship was going to end, then I at least deserved a chance to speak my mind. "I saw how beautiful she was, Jorge. Gorgeous! Let me guess, she's a supermodel on the side, isn't she? And to think that I started developing feelings for you! I never should have done that accounting work for you, either!"

"Ginger, I am begging you to tell me where all of this is coming from."

Fed up with his lies, I threw my purse onto the sidewalk out of frustration. "I saw you pull into the parking lot with her in your car last week, Jorge. And the two of you went into your building!"

Of course, Jorge looked surprised, because he had thought that I was busy at work.

"That's right, I bet you didn't think I'd find out! Well, guess what? I took the afternoon off because I couldn't stop thinking about you!"

"Ginger, I didn't have sex with her that day. I haven't had sex with her in months, and I'm begging you to believe me."

"Then why the hell did she fly to Miami? Was I not good enough for you? Was the sex too lackluster or something?"

Jorge took my hand, grabbed my purse off the ground, and walked me over to a nearby bench. I reluctantly sat down and snatched my bag from his hand.

"She flew back to Miami to discuss the accounting errors that you found. The only reason I brought her to my place was that I didn't want to be seen with her in public. She's staying at her place, and I haven't seen her since she left that day in a huff."

My heart rate started to slow down as I took in what he was saying. "Why did she leave in a huff?"

"Because I told her that I never had feelings for her, Ginger, and I never have."

A few people walking into the restaurant stopped to look at us, but I didn't care.

"So, you really didn't sleep with her? You were just trying to get her to leave the business?"

He nodded while rubbing his fingers over my hand. "Look, Ginger, yes, she does want me back, and she actually thought that one day I'd propose to her. Needless to say, that won't be happening, and now she knows."

It felt like a cloud had been lifted from over me. "I– I'm so sorry! I had no idea. I just assumed when I saw her get out... I should have trusted you."

Jorge kissed me, causing my knees to go weak. "You have nothing to be sorry about, Ginger. I'm the one who should be apologizing."

"So, how are you going to get her to go back to Belgium?"

"Well, I think she finally believes that I'm in love with another woman. After a few choice words, which I'll spare you from hearing, she seems to understand our relationship was really only a matter of convenience... for both of us."

I leaned back and looked into his eyes, confused. "Wait, you're in love with another woman?"

Jorge chuckled while shaking his head at me. "Ginger, the other woman is *you*. I'm in love with you."

"Oh, Jorge, I'm in love with you, too. I'm so sorry about not trusting you." We embraced on the bench, wrapping our arms around each other as people looked on from inside the restaurant. I didn't care, though.

I was finally back with Jorge. Chase and Eva walked outside as soon as we stopped kissing several minutes later, both of them visibly relieved the drama was over.

Chase shook his head while slow clapping. "Have you two finally worked things out yet?"

"Yeah," Eva said while smiling, "are you guys all right now?"

Jorge nodded while kissing me again, then squeezing my hand. "We're fine, but there's just one more thing that I might need you to do for me."

I gazed into his eyes while smiling. "Anything for you, Jorge."

He tilted his head and grinned. "Can you be my fake fiancée for a day?"

12

Jorge

After everything I'd gone through with Ria and Ginger, I took full advantage of working from home. There was nothing better than sliding out of bed and shuffling into my office, where I could get work done without any interference from my employees. But that morning, as I signed onto my laptop, with a coffee in hand, I saw yet another email from the De Veers Diamond Group.

Before I opened it, I knew it had to do with the wages of our workers in Africa and the union was calling for a strike.

I waited for the coffee to finish brewing before reading it. I needed to be fully caffeinated before dealing with this fiasco, which Ria should have taken care of back when it first came up. She was holding out on purpose. Ria was fully aware that I was far too busy to deal with this part of the business, which was pretty much all she was in charge of. She knew what the going rates were for diamond-mine workers and what their unions were like. I didn't even know what the working conditions were like down in Africa.

I read it while downing my first coffee cup, and sure enough, they wanted more money. I hadn't heard anything from Ria ever since she had stormed out of my penthouse, but she was signing in to work every day and still doing her job. I decided to give her some time to come to her senses because the last thing I wanted to do was get my lawyers involved. Watching her leave so upset had been the icing on the cake because I knew I'd finally gotten through to her.

But now that I had another situation on my hands, I needed Ria to do her job.

She had all of the files regarding our employees in Africa. I simply couldn't authorize anything more without going over them in detail, and I knew she wouldn't give them over to me. It'd be a huge red flag that I was, whether she liked it or not, axing her from the company.

I thought about what to do as my fingers hovered over the mouse. Realizing I had no other choice, I forwarded it to Ria.

Ria,

Please take care of this ASAP. We cannot afford to have these workers on strike for too long. A friendly reminder that I took care of it last time. Since you have all of the necessary documentation and are still on the payroll, make sure you give them a big enough raise so this doesn't happen again. But not so much that we're paying them more than the industry standard.

Sincerely,

Jorge

I hit the "send" button and waited for a response.

To keep my mind occupied, I decided to call Gavin and let him know that I was finally trying to buy out Ria. "Good morning," I said as he groggily picked up.

"Why are you up so early?"

"It's eight-thirty in the morning. Aren't you back in Florida for a few weeks? Or did I catch you on California time?" I refreshed my computer screen, but still no response from Ria.

"Yeah, I'm in town for a few weeks, but my body is still on California time. I don't have to be at my agent's office until noon."

"Well, I just wanted to let you know that you were right about Ria. Ginger looked over the books for me, since she's an accountant, and found that Ria embezzled nearly a million bucks."

The sound of a mug crashing onto the counter roared through the telephone. "Did you just say a million dollars? Dude, I told you she was bad news!"

I double-checked her status on our office instant messaging system, but it said she wasn't available. She hadn't been on it since our big blowout, either.

"She wouldn't accept my offer to buy her out of our partnership. I'm just giving her some time to calm down after we had a big fight the other day." I kept refreshing my email, even though I knew it wasn't necessary. My penthouse had the fastest internet speed available.

"Is she still trying to sleep with you?"

"She's doing more than just that, Gavin. Ria is expecting me to propose to her, which I made abundantly clear would never, ever happen."

"I can't imagine that went over well."

"Nope, and now I'm waiting for her to reply to an email regarding work. Normally I'd take care of it myself, but only she has access to the necessary information. Plus, it'll take some time to go over everything, and that's one thing I don't have today. I have four, one-hour conference calls, plus I have to make myself somewhat presentable for a business lunch with a potential client."

"Keep me in the loop. You're doing the right thing, though. Speaking of which, I have to find some time to see my daughter while I'm in town. Maybe you and I could do lunch sometime too."

The loud ping of an incoming email shifted my focus back to work. "Absolutely. Let me take care of this Ria nonsense, first, though. In fact, she just emailed me. I'll text you later on." I took a long, deep breath while double-clicking her response.

Good morning, Jorge,

I knew you'd need me eventually.

You're in quite the predicament right now, aren't you? Without the diamond miners working, you could lose a tremendous amount of money—no need to worry, though. I know what it'll take to prevent them from ever striking again.

I'm more than willing to take care of this for you, mainly since I know you have an incredibly busy day, but on one condition—I get to meet your fiancée tonight.

Sincerely,

Ria

P.S.: You might be the best when it comes to spotting fake diamonds, but I'm the best when it comes to spotting fake men.

I slammed my laptop shut while screaming some obscenities.

I knew she wouldn't go away quietly!

The good news was that Ginger was on-board with being my fake fiancée. The bad news was that I didn't know how drawn out this whole thing would be. It was one thing to pretend to be engaged but a whole other ballgame trying to pull off a fake wedding.

I called Ginger, even though I knew she'd be at work.

"Good morning, handsome. How's your day going?"

I slumped in my chair, preparing myself to tell her that it was time. "That depends on how you respond to this question. Is tonight a good night to be my fake fiancée?"

I knew Ginger would go silent for a few seconds, but not an entire minute. I stared at the clock on my laptop, watching the seconds tick until she finally answered.

"Yeah, that's fine." Her voice was clipped, and suddenly I wasn't so sure.

"Actually, maybe I should just have my lawyers take care of this Ginger. It's not fair to ask you to do such a thing, and Ria really is intuitive. She might pick up that I'm lying, and it'll only make everything worse."

"Jorge, I have every intention of looking Ria right in the face and telling her that we're engaged. I thought about it after our conversation the other day, and you're right: this probably is the better way to go. And don't worry about my being convincing. I took a few acting classes back in college." I chuckled while picturing her playing Lady Macbeth. "Oh, crap. I can't do it tonight."

"Why not?"

"Guadalupe and Yuslan are implementing a new software system, and I have to merge all of the data onto the new one. It has something to do with it going out of business. Anyway, what about tomorrow night?"

Crap! Ria is not very flexible.

But I realized that I had to man-up eventually. "I'll make sure that it happens tomorrow night, no problem."

"Thank you! And I'm sorry about tonight, but it has to get done. Crap, I gotta get back to work now."

"All right, sounds good. Let me email Ria back, and then I'll text you all of the details. I love you."

"I love you too."

Despite having been with numerous women, I had never told anyone but Ginger that I loved her. And it felt amazing.

I took a long, deep breath and replied to Ria.

Ria,

Tonight's not good. Even you acknowledged that I have a busy day. (Please stop getting my schedule from my secretary, by the way.) Tomorrow night, six o'clock, at The Spicy Pineapple for drinks. If you don't accept this time and place, I'll move forward with getting my lawyers involved.

Sincerely,

Jorge

Ria took her sweet time in getting back to me, which drove me insane, but I also appreciated not having to deal with her. I answered another few emails that demanded my immediate attention, all the while nervous about her response. At that point, Ria was likely to be so pissed off that she'd just say, "screw it" and screw me over altogether.

I breathed a sigh of relief when she finally emailed me back thirty minutes later.

Jorge,

I authorized a small increase in wages to employees in the African diamond mines. They've agreed to resume mining, but not for too much longer. It'd be a shame if I didn't give them everything they wanted and they just up and quit their jobs.

See you tomorrow night.

Sincerely,

Ria

Feeling relieved at having dodged a major landmine, I called my secretary and rescheduled all of my conference calls and business lunch that day. I also forbid her from telling anything about me or the company to Ria. And being the great secretary that she was, she agreed without asking for any details. As for Ria's threat about making the workers quit their jobs, which would cost me a tremendous amount of money, I knew Ginger and I could pull it off.

You're about to be history, Ria.

13

Ginger

Every outfit in my closet was screaming my name. I would be meeting Ria that night, and I needed to look as fabulous as possible. I hadn't gotten the best look at her when she had climbed out of Jorge's convertible, especially with those obnoxiously large sunglasses covering most of her face, but the parts I did get a look at were...nice. Ria probably turned a lot of heads, if only for the way she dressed. That leopard mini-skirt and white halter top couldn't have been any sluttier, especially for a so-called business meeting with Jorge.

She had every intention of sleeping with him that afternoon too.

I didn't need all of the details from their meeting to get a sense of what had happened. I was sure Ria was all over him, using her sexuality to convince him that she had never so much as embezzled a dime. And now that I knew I could trust Jorge, I was ready to put her in her place. I wouldn't tell her that I was the one who discovered she'd been lying to him, but I would say that he was mine and that she needed to leave him alone.

I decided on a yellow dress that stopped just a few inches above the knee. It was classy enough to stand out against Ria's promiscuous outfits but sexy enough to arouse Jorge. After sliding into the dress and touching up my makeup, I wrapped the diamond tennis bracelet around my wrist and snapped it shut. Ria would take one look at it and automatically know who it was from.

Just as I slid into my favorite pair of nude high heels, Jorge rang my doorbell.

"You look gorgeous," he said while handing me a dozen roses.

"Jorge, these are beautiful!"

I put them into a vase with some water, and then we sat down in the living room to discuss the plan.

"A couple of things you need to know about Ria. First of all, she's conniving. Expect her to ask you condescending questions that'll throw you for a loop."

"Can you give me an example?"

"Yes, but please don't be offended by anything that I say." Urging him to continue, I shook my head. "Well, she'll probably look at your dress and ask you what discount store you got it from."

"Excuse me? This dress cost me five-hundred-dollars!" Jorge took my hand, and that's all that was needed to bring me back down to earth. "Sorry, please go on. What other things will she ask?"

"In addition to dodging her nasty remarks about your clothes, she's going to want to know our relationship details. Say that we've known for a while that we belong together. Oh, and that I proposed to you at your party."

"I can do that, except for one little problem." I held out my ring finger, which was missing an engagement ring.

Jorge pulled a box from his pocket, opened it up, and showed me one of the most beautiful diamonds I'd ever seen. "No worries, I brought something with me from work. One of the perks of being in the diamond industry."

I tried to remain calm as he slid it onto my finger, reminding myself that it was all pretend. Jorge and I weren't engaged. Hell, we had literally just become a couple a few weeks ago.

Then why am I so excited about playing his fiancée tonight?

"It's gorgeous, Jorge. Speaking of gorgeous, can you show me a better picture of her?"

He pulled up a picture on his cell phone, which gave me a more unobstructed view of her face. Ria was a knockout.

"As you can see, she's had far too much plastic surgery on her face. She still thinks she's pretty, though."

"*Thinks* she's pretty? Jorge, she's gorgeous. Take a look at those cheekbones, those lips, and those eyelashes!"

Jorge chuckled while putting his phone away. "All of it is fake, Ginger, right down to the eyelashes."

"What about her breasts?"

"Not only are they also fake, but they're hard as a rock. Sorry, I'm sure you don't want to hear that part."

Knowing the two of them had been intimate no longer bothered me. All that mattered was that Jorge and I were together, and Ria would soon be a thing of the past.

"No, it's fine. That actually makes me feel better. So, assuming that Ria believes all of this, what's your game plan?"

"That she'll believe we're engaged, get over me, accept my offer of buying her out, and take care of the issue with the De Veers Diamond Group before I look to fill her position."

"Will it be hard to find someone?"

Jorge seemed optimistic. "No, not really. But the mess with De Veers needs to be handled before she leaves the company. When it comes to our diamond workers in Africa, it's not as simple as giving them a raise."

"Gotcha."

We arrived at the restaurant exactly at five minutes to six. The hostess sat us down at a table right near the door, which gave us the perfect view of Ria walking into the restaurant. I was feeling fine until she waltzed in wearing an incredibly form-fitting red dress and black high heels.

If I didn't know any better, I'd assume she was a movie star.

Ria slid into the other side of the booth without even looking at me. "Good evening, Jorge."

I cleared my voice before speaking. "Good evening, Ria. I'm Ginger."

She merely nodded while looking over the menu.

Jorge was in no mood to play games. "We're not ordering food tonight, Ria. Order a drink on me, and let's get this over with."

She slammed the menu shut, placed a drink order with the server, and glared at me. "How much do I have to pay you, Ginger?"

"Excuse me?"

"You heard me. Look, you're only interested in Jorge for his money but not me. That's because I come from money, darling."

I started to stand up, but Jorge tightened his grip on my hand. "Let's get one thing straight, Ria. I called off my engagement with Jorge when I thought he was hooking up with you. So believe me, the last thing I'm after is money."

She looked at Jorge, who smiled and nodded.

I kept going, "I knew Jorge was the one for me several months ago, when we talked on the phone, and he listened intently as I poured my heart out. I was stressed about school, worried about the future, and he was the one I could count on."

Jorge looked at me with shock in his eyes, and I realized that I'd just spilled my guts to him.

Ria, on the other hand, smirked. "What a sweet story, darling—"

"Ginger," I said. "My name is Ginger, not darling."

She took a long sip of her drink while rolling her eyes. "Whatever, Ginger. How long have you two known each other?"

"Well, he was a good friend of my brother's back in college, but we were reintroduced last year at a wedding reception." Ginger looked at Jorge and then back at me.

"And what do you do for a living?"

"That's none of your business, Ria."

She rolled her eyes while taking another sip of her drink. "All right, prove to me that you know Jorge as well as I do. How does he take his coffee?"

"One cream."

"Favorite meal?"

"Fried chicken."

"Favorite sexual position?"

Jorge wasn't having any of that talk that night. "No, Ginger. This is getting out of hand. What more do you want out of me? We're engaged!"

Ria protruded her fake breasts out in defiance. "Show me the engagement ring."

Jorge let go of my left hand so I could show it to her. Ria yanked my fingers closer to her face, where she scrutinized it to make sure it was real. It took her several minutes of zooming in and out with her eyes, looking for any indication that it was a fake.

When she was done, she threw my hand to the table so hard that I winced in pain.

"Ow," I yelled while using my right hand to massage my

left wrist. That was when Ria's eyes lit up at the diamond tennis bracelet around my right wrist.

She went to grab it, but Jorge stopped her.

"Keep your damn hands off of my fiancée, Ria!"

Water welled up in her eyes as she looked at both of us. "You gave her a diamond tennis bracelet, Jorge?"

"Yes, I did. Why?"

Ria grabbed her purse and stood up. "Not once, in all of our years together, have you ever given me a piece of jewelry! You want me gone? Well, here's your goodbye! Good luck with this bastard, Ginger! You're gonna need it."

Ria pushed through the restaurant's doors as everyone watched, wondering what the hell had just happened.

By the time Jorge and I got back to my place, we were all over each other. At every red light, we made out, and I couldn't keep my hands off him while driving. As we made our way into my condo, we were ripping each other's clothes off to see who could get naked the fastest.

Our hot, nude bodies tumbled onto my bed, rolling around as we pressed up against each other. My hard nipples pushed against Jorge's muscular chest, and I could feel the heat intensify between our groins.

"I love you so much," he whispered before laying me onto my back. As we locked hands, he slid his thick, massive cock deep inside of me. It still blew me away at how big he was, which was significantly more so than any man I'd ever been with. Every inch of him filled me up, causing my back to arch as he pounded away.

"Oh, God, Jorge!"

He answered my cries of ecstasy by sucking on my hardened nipples, thrusting even harder as our bodies became one. I couldn't remember the last time I had been so wet.

Every time I climbed on top of him, we held hands, and he really gripped my fake engagement ring. I had thought about taking it off as soon as Ria had left the restaurant, but it felt so right on my finger. I also loved the idea of wearing it while he had his arm wrapped around my waist. Even though we'd just started going out, I wanted people to think that we really were engaged.

I leaned forward to kiss him, and as I leaned back against his cock he caressed my left hand and and ran his thumb over the diamond ring.

God, that is so hot!

I leaned back, and he climbed on top, pumping in and out of me as I wrapped my legs around his waist. It was, without a doubt, the hottest sex we'd ever had. He sucked my nipples harder than before, which only caused me to become even wetter. And every time I squeezed his shaft with my lips, he let out a loud moan that was so deep I almost came.

We spent the next hour just rolling around on my bed, and not once did he pull out of me. We even tried a couple of new positions, and one of my favorites was being bent over the bed. I especially loved the feeling of his heavy balls slapping against my clit while he moaned my name.

Jorge laid on his back toward the end of our lovemaking, allowing me to run my nails up and down his chest as I rode him to completion. The two of us never lost eye contact as we came to a finish, both of us climaxing so hard that I was sure my mirrors would shatter. And when it was all over, we fell asleep in each other's arms.

I couldn't help but notice how many times Jorge ran his fingers over my fake engagement ring, too, which I never took off. And when I woke up the next morning, he was holding my left hand and focusing on the diamond.

14

Jorge

I didn't know what time we had fallen asleep after making love, but it must have been within minutes. Even though I was in excellent physical shape, Ginger and I had practically ravished each other the second we had gotten in the door. It took all of my willpower not to bury myself deep inside of her right there in her hallway. Between telling Ria off and seeing her wear the fake engagement ring, I knew that Ginger and I would become inseparable.

That was the longest I'd ever had sex with someone, and it was also the most fulfilling. The way Ginger's body perfectly melded with mine was unlike anything I'd ever experienced, and I was starting to appreciate her more than before. Not that sex with her had never been spectacular, though.

While pumping away for nearly an hour, not once breaking our connection, it finally felt as though my life were complete. And as I rolled over the next morning and saw Ginger laying next to me, with our hands intertwined, I knew there was no other place I'd rather be.

As I lay in bed while watching her sleep for several minutes, I breathed a sigh of relief that Ria was finally out of our lives. Of course, I'd still have to deal with the business part of her leaving the company. That would be addressed in the next several weeks. But after seeing the look on her face as she left the restaurant, it couldn't have been clearer that I'd gotten through to her.

Then again, Ria had always been one to play mind games. There was a chance that her walking out in such a dramatic way was all for show, and she'd find some way to sneak back into my life. It was highly unlikely, though. In all of the years that she and I had known each other, I'd never seen her look as upset as she did when she saw the tennis bracelet.

My biggest concern had been for Ginger. It was one thing for me to deal with Ria, but Ginger shouldn't have to put up with anything that evil woman had done. She was far too sweet and innocent. Now that Ria was out of the picture, my future with Ginger had a green light. But I also knew that I couldn't keep putting Ginger through so much crap just so we could be rid of Ria and be together.

Ginger had done a beautiful job of decorating her condo. That was my first thought as I made my way into her bathroom and found a spare toothbrush underneath the sink. Our tastes in decor were almost identical—clean, modern lines with colorful accents. I often found contemporary to be too harsh too. Almost industrial-like. My next idea was that when we moved in together, we probably wouldn't bicker over how to design each room.

Move-in with Ginger? We just started dating!

I splashed some cold water onto my face, realizing that I was getting ahead of myself. I had never been in a serious, long-term relationship before, and there I was thinking about us moving in together. It was impossible not to at least consider it, though, after being wrapped up in each other's arms all night long.

As I washed up that morning, I couldn't help but feel like I'd suddenly become a man. Sure, I was a successful diamond broker worth billions, but all that meant was that I had money. Until I'd reunited with Ginger after spending a year apart, I had thought that was enough, especially since I could have my choice of just about any woman I wanted. But after making love to Ginger the night before, I had started to appreciate our emotional connection.

I had to start my day in a few minutes, and Ginger would be getting up soon. So, I brewed a full pot of coffee for both of us. The freshly ground Colombian beans made the entire condo smell delightful. And when it finished brewing, I decided to watch Ginger sleeping while enjoying a cup from the doorway.

She looked so peaceful curled up in bed, with her hair spread all over the pillows. Ginger was on her back with her arms outstretched, which meant she had probably moved once I had gotten out of bed. I could have stood there all morning and watched her sleep, her soft, delicate bosom moving up and down with every breath. One look at my watch, though, and I knew that I needed to leave. I still couldn't put my finger on it, but there was something even more beautiful about her that morning.

I wrote a quick note to Ginger, explaining why I had to go, and when I went to put it on the nightstand, she'd since rolled onto her stomach. I chuckled while putting it next to her alarm clock, and that's when it hit me: she had never removed the engagement ring.

Images of us making love the night before flooded my mind, and I remembered continually rubbing my fingers over that ring as we rolled around on her bed. If I'd asked any other woman to be my fake fiancée, I'd have slipped the diamond off her finger the second we had left the restaurant, knowing its value. But that never even occurred to me with Ginger.

I started to lean forward, realizing that the ring would have to come off eventually. After all, we weren't actually engaged. But the closer my hands got to the ring, the more hesitant I became.

So, I kissed her on the forehead and went back to my penthouse.

What would she think if she woke up and the ring was gone?

I booted up my laptop as soon as I got back home. On some level, I started to feel guilty about not working from my office in downtown Miami. But I loved the peace and quiet that came with working from home. Plus, it meant that nobody could hear me scream obscenities upon seeing all of my emails.

That morning, however, was pleasantly different. There were only five hundred emails as opposed to the usual thousand or so, and I enjoyed another cup of coffee while scanning them over.

Some of them needed my immediate attention, such as the ones from my secretary, but most of them could wait until later. I felt pretty good about the day ahead, especially since there were no emails from the De Veers Diamond Group. All I needed to do was plow through all of them, make a few phone calls, and relax with Ginger that evening.

And then I saw the email from Ria, and it had nothing to do with business.

Jorge,

I only left last night because I couldn't believe you'd buy Ginger a diamond tennis bracelet to "prove" you're engaged. Perhaps you've forgotten that I know everything there is to know about you. For starters, you are not *the marrying type. Maybe you have butterflies in your stomach with Ginger like you did with me when we first met. But what you're feeling isn't love.*

The way you two were fawning all over each other was over the top and dramatic. I'm sure everyone else at The Spicy Pineapple knew you were putting on a show for me. You might be able to spot a fake diamond, but you can't pull off a fake engagement.

Oh, and that so-called ring you got her is hideous and obnoxious.

Anyway, don't bother calling or emailing me all day because I'm up to my ears with work.

Sincerely,

Ria

I paced back and forth at my desk for several minutes, furious that she still didn't get it. Before getting my lawyers involved, I decided to call her one last time.

"Didn't I make it perfectly clear that I was swamped with work today, Jorge?"

"Bullshit. We both know that you're sitting at home, waiting for this call because of the email you sent me. You got your wish, Ria! You met Ginger, saw the engagement ring, and even saw the tennis bracelet that I bought for *her*—which by the way, was a graduation present. Even you acknowledged that not once during our 'relationship' did I ever buy you jewelry. So please, for the love of God, Ria, why won't you accept that we're over?"

She let out an obnoxious chuckle, and I could just envision her lipstick-stained teeth sneering into the phone. "There's nothing to accept, Jorge. You and I are meant to be together. And the more you carry on with this charade, the more I'll dig in my heels."

"Are you actually telling me that you still don't believe that I'm engaged?"

"Precisely, Jorge. Remember when I said that I'd wasted the best years of my life on you? I wasn't kidding. So if you think that I'm going back into the dating scene after all of our time—"

"You were nothing but someone to have sex with, Ria! Do you understand that? And you weren't even that good!" Criticizing Ria's sexual skills was about the worst thing I could have done.

"Screw you, Jorge! If I weren't so good, you would have stopped having sex with me a long time ago! But you kept coming back for more!"

"You and I both know that's not what happened, Ria. From day one, you were all over me, and if memory serves me correctly, I tried keeping you at bay."

"Then how come you were always flirting with me, Jorge?"

"Please, Ria. You were the one always coming onto me. Any man with a functioning penis would have given in to you. It has nothing to do with your looks or how you perform in bed, either. But enough about this because I'm serious about dissolving our partnership. My offer still stands, Ria: five hundred million dollars, and I won't get my lawyers involved."

She laughed so hard into the phone that I could just picture her tilting back her head.

You crazy, maniacal, sadistic thief!

"Oh, Jorge. Something tells me that I have more money than you do. I just don't feel the need to prove it to everyone that I meet. Now, if you'll excuse me, I have to get back to work."

"No, Ria! Don't you dare hang up this phone! I want you to go on back to Antwerp; do you hear me? Go back to your friends and family and enjoy being retired for a while! Go back and forget about me."

Her long nails started drumming against a hard surface, which was a sound that I was beginning to despise. "If you really wanted me out of your life, Jorge, then you wouldn't be calling me. You wouldn't have gone through all of this just to prove to me that you're engaged. You would have gone straight to your lawyers because you're not really concerned about me ruining your reputation in the diamond community...right?"

Ria hung up the phone, and I punched the "end call" button so hard on mine that it nearly cracked the screen. My mind was racing a mile a minute as I tried to figure out a plan. Ria had officially gone off of the deep end, that was for damn sure. Realizing that I'd need some outside help, I called Gavin, who was in town filming a movie.

"You have to stop with these early morning wake-up calls, man."

"Ria's bat-shit crazy, Gavin, and I'm really starting to freak out. I can't believe that I ever got involved with her in the first place."

The sound of him shuffling out of bed filled the phone, and I pictured him heading toward his coffee machine.

"If I had a dollar for every time I said 'I told you so' about Ria, I'd be up to my ears in singles. Anyway, what the hell did she do now?"

"She insisted on meeting my fiancée, but after meeting Ginger and me for drinks and seeing her engagement ring, Ria's still not convinced!"

"Whoa, you're engaged?"

My heart started beating even faster, but this time with excitement. I suddenly pictured Ginger walking down the aisle in a wedding gown, smiling at me while holding onto a bouquet.

Calm down, Jorge.

"No, of course not. We just started dating. But I had Ginger wear a ring for emphasis. Anyway, Ria's refusing to leave the company! What do I do?"

"Well, that depends. What else did Ria say, man?"

"She said that I'm not the marrying type and that she refuses to go back into the dating pool after 'wasting' the best years of her life on me."

Gavin sat in silence for a few minutes, which only added to my irritation. "So, Ria's looking to become your wife?"

"Yep."

"I might be drowsy as hell, Jorge, but it's pretty obvious what you need to do: have an actual wedding ceremony."

I nearly passed out in my home office. "What the hell are you talking about, Gavin?"

"Until Ria sees you and Ginger exchange vows, she's not going to leave you alone."

I slowly sat down in my seat, realizing that he was one hundred percent right. "Holy shit, Gavin. That makes total sense. Oh, God. This is a nightmare."

"Tell Ginger to hold onto that engagement ring, and that it's time to start looking for a wedding dress."

15

Ginger

I was a little sad not to see Jorge laying next to me in bed that morning, but his note on my dresser put a smile on my face. I was also thrilled that we'd finally gotten rid of Ria, once and for all. As I slipped into a peach-silk dress and studied myself in the mirror, my eyes immediately gravitated to the engagement ring. It would have been fun wearing it to work all day, but Guadalupe would demand to know all of the details. And I just wasn't in the mood to explain the fake-fiancée storyline.

There's no harm in wearing it while driving into work, though.

I decided to take the long way to the spa that day, intentionally resting my left hand on the edge of my window at every red light. Even though I never looked to see the people in the cars next to me, I caught several women in my peripheral vision eyeing my engagement ring.

Maybe I'll wear it at work, after all.

By the time I slid into my chair and booted up my computer, though, the ring was tucked firmly away in my purse. If I weren't afraid of Guadalupe popping her head into my office, I might have worked an hour or so with it on. But she loved to make her morning rounds to everyone in the spa, checking in to make sure we were all in a good mood. And if we weren't, then she'd shove one of her miniature cakes into our mouths.

And just when I thought about wearing it for another few minutes, Guadalupe stuck her motherly head in to say hello.

"Good morning, darling! I hope you're in a good mood today."

"Of course I am, Guadalupe. Please don't come in here with any of those cakes, though. My jeans are already feeling a little too tight lately!"

She chuckled while resting the platter of miniature cakes on an end table next to my door. "Okay, okay. But as soon as your jeans loosen up, you're eating one of these. Are you busy right now, or do you have a few minutes?" Guadalupe had never been one to ask if any of us had a few minutes. She was practically our mother, and if she wanted to talk to you about something, then she did. So whatever she needed me for, it was clearly important.

I tensed up a little bit, even though I knew it probably wouldn't be anything terrible. Everything had been going well at the spa, and to my knowledge, I hadn't done anything wrong. Still, being called into your boss's office elicited a sense of worry.

"Sure, I have a few minutes. Is everything all right, or am I in trouble?"

She smiled while inviting me to follow her. Every employee we passed in the spa stared at me with fear in their eyes, clearly wondering why I was behind Guadalupe. I'd never seen her pull anyone into her office before. By the time I sat down in front of her desk, I was a ball of nerves.

Yuslan came in after us and patted me on the back. "Why do you look so worried, dear?"

I smiled at him while trying to calm myself down, which wasn't working. "Oh, it's nothing. I guess I'm just concerned that I did something wrong."

Both of them chuckled, and Yuslan reassured me there was nothing to worry about. "Darling, we wouldn't have promoted you if we didn't think you'd be good. In fact, Guadalupe and I talked about you last night, and we've decided to give you a twenty-percent raise!"

I nearly fell out of my chair. "Wait. What? Are you serious? But I just started!"

Guadalupe reached across the desk and clutched both of my hands. "The woman before you was nice, but we were always coming across errors in her work. But with you, Ginger, it's the complete opposite. Plus, we know how expensive living in a big city like Miami can be. And you've been with Lavender Dreams Spa longer than in your current position. Most of the clients recognize you, and you always go out of your way to make them feel at home."

I started fanning my face as tears ran down my cheeks. "I just can't thank you two enough! Twenty percent is so much, though! Are you sure?"

"We're more than sure, Ginger. Oh, and you also get an extra two weeks of vacation per year with this raise. That's in addition to your current two weeks, making it a total of four weeks. You'll also get a larger percentage in our profit sharing, paid holidays, and unlimited sick days."

"I don't even know what to say, you guys! This is so unexpected! I'm really getting four weeks of vacation?"

"Yes," Guadalupe said with a smile, "which is perfect timing because now you can travel with your tall, dark, and handsome man! Just be sure to bring me back something from wherever you guys visit because, with him, I just know it'll be someplace fabulous!"

I giggled as she clutched her hands to her heart. Yuslan chuckled while handing me an envelope, as he always found his wife to be quite funny. I opened it up to find a five-thousand-dollar bonus check.

"This is a little something extra to help with your student loans, dear."

I was crying so hard that I knew I'd have to reapply my makeup, but it was all worth it. Guadalupe and Yuslan had just made it possible to pay off my student loans in almost half the time.

"Thank you, thank you, thank you!"

All three of us hugged, and by the time I got back to my desk, I knew I would never leave the Lavender Dreams Spa. I immediately called Margo, who was at home, and by the sounds of it, nursing baby Joanna.

"Good morning, Ginger! How are things at the spa today?"

"Guadalupe and Yuslan just gave me a twenty-percent raise, plus a huge bonus check!"

"Oh, that's wonderful, Ginger! We have to go out and celebrate tonight!"

As soon as she said the word "celebrate," I immediately got excited about wearing the fake engagement ring.

"Yes! Oh God, this is going to be so much fun! How about The Spicy Pineapple?"

"That sounds great. I haven't been there before, though. Have you?"

A smirk played across my face as I remembered seeing Ria storm out of there the night before. "Oh, yes. In fact, Jorge and I were there last night. I'll tell you and Eva all about it over drinks."

The Spicy Pineapple was full of people that night, especially at the bar. Luckily, we were able to snag three empty seats next to each other. As soon as we sat down, Eva's eyes lit up while staring at my engagement ring.

"Ginger, did Jorge actually propose to you?" Margo reached over and yanked my hand to her face, studying it as carefully as Ria had done.

Eva's jaw dropped. "Oh, my God! I thought it was all an act, Ginger! When are you two getting married?"

I chuckled while shaking my head at both of them. "No, I just like wearing it. Besides, Jorge hasn't asked for it back yet."

"So," Eva said while sipping her glass of merlot, "how did it go with Ria?"

"First of all, she's absolutely gorgeous."

"Oh, stop," Margo said. "I bet she's nothing compared to you. Besides, Chase told me that she's all butchered up from so much cosmetic surgery."

"Well, that's true. Ria has had a lot of work done, and it shows. But she really is pretty. Anyway, she was a total snob to me from the second she sat down at our booth. She kept asking condescending questions, and even after she saw the ring still didn't believe we were engaged!"

Eva rolled her eyes. "That woman is so obsessed with Jorge that he's having a hard time getting rid of her. So, what made her believe it then?"

"Ria threw my hand onto the table so hard that it hurt, and when I went to rub it with my left hand, she saw the diamond tennis bracelet and lost her damn mind. She ripped into Jorge, telling him that in all of their time together, not once did he ever give her a piece of jewelry!"

Margo burst out laughing. "I think that sums up her relationship with Jorge. Then what happened?"

"Well, she stormed right out of here while everyone in the restaurant watched. Even the poor hostess nearly got trampled as she tried leaving. I'm telling you, that woman is batshit crazy. Although, seeing her get so worked up was the most satisfying thing I have ever witnessed."

Margo shook her head while continuing to laugh. "And to top it off, you had an incredible day at the spa this morning! I still can't believe Guadalupe and Yuslan did that to you so soon after your promotion."

Eva's eyes bugged out as she looked at Margo and then me, whipping her head back and forth. "Oh, my God! What happened at the salon? Tell me, Ginger!"

I laughed at Eva, who seemed more excited than I was. "Yuslan and Guadalupe gave me a raise, plus a bonus. But don't tell anyone else at work."

Eva clapped her hands together while bouncing up and down in her seat. Several people at the bar looked at her and laughed, wondering why she was so exciting. "Oh, that's wonderful, Ginger! Everything is going so well in your life!"

Finally.

"Thank you. I'm just so happy to not only feel secure in my career, but also in my relationship with Jorge. Sure, the engagement ring was fake—in sentiment, not quality—and I'll give it back to him the next time we get together. But after last night, everything just felt so...right."

Margo shook her head at me while smiling. "I bet you're going to keep that engagement ring, and I guarantee Jorge is going to propose!"

Eva clutched her heart. "Oh, I bet she will too! Maybe he'll reenact something from a movie. But nothing too cheesy, of course. Jorge is a classy guy."

I doubled over with laughter. "You guys, we've only been dating for a few weeks. It's way too soon! And I'm only wearing it because it's so pretty. Plus, it matches my diamond tennis bracelet." I held both of them up in the air, close together.

"Well," Eva said, "I don't think Ria will be bothering you anymore. That woman got exactly what she deserved."

We spent the rest of the evening catching up on gossip, and I couldn't remember the last time I'd felt so complete. Everything in my life was finally coming together.

And when I went to bed that night, I wore both the tennis bracelet and the engagement ring.

16

Jorge

"Right this way, Mr. Stein."

The hostess at Seafood Divine showed me to our table, located on their outside terrace right alongside the ocean. I'd chosen that restaurant to celebrate Ginger's recent promotion because she loved seafood, and their cheese-stuffed lobster was some of the best I'd ever tasted. I also wanted to butter her up enough so that she'd say "yes" to being my fake bride, during our phony wedding ceremony.

Usually, I'd wait for Ginger to arrive before drinking, but I downed a whiskey neat right before she sat down. My nerves were officially shot from the argument with Ria and trying to come up with a plan to pull off a fake wedding ceremony. I kept repeating my speech over in my head.

So, listen, Ginger. Do you remember how Ria just up and stormed out of The Spicy Pineapple? Well, as it turns out, she still doesn't believe that we're engaged. We'll have to throw a fake ceremony, too. Is that going to be a problem?

"I might as well dig my own grave right now."

The waitress turned her head in my direction while walking toward another table. "I'm sorry, Mr. Stein. What did you say?"

"Oh, nothing. I'm just mumbling to myself."

"Would you like another drink?"

Yes, but only because I'll need to be wasted to get through this evening.

"No, that's all right. I'll wait for my date and then we'll have champagne. Thank you for asking, though."

As it got closer to fifteen minutes past our scheduled time, I was starting to worry about Ginger. I was also starting to become self-conscious about everyone staring at me, probably wondering why I was sitting all alone at a table for two. My mind started racing, wondering if Ria had shown up at the Lavender Dreams Spa to confront Ginger.

That's something she would do.

Right as I was about to call Ginger, she arrived and sat down, clearly out of breath.

"I'm so sorry that I'm late," Ginger said while opening up her menu. "Guadalupe and I were discussing a few things about the salon, and I didn't want to rush her by saying that I had to leave. She's like a mother to me. I was going to call or text you, but traffic was awful, and I can't figure out how to work my hands-free option while driving."

I picked her left hand up, brought it to my mouth, and kissed her finger right above the diamond ring. "You never have to apologize to me, Ginger. Believe me. I completely understand about running late due to work. And I can show you how to work your Bluetooth after we eat tonight if you'd like."

Our waitress brought over a bottle of their most expensive champagne, popped it open, and then poured each of us a glass.

"To your new promotion at Lavender Dreams Spa."

Ginger looked breathtaking as she studied the menu, especially as the candlelight flickered against her gorgeous auburn hair.

"Everything looks so good here. I can't decide between the calamari or one of the shrimp platters."

"I highly recommend the lobster. The cheese melts between the succulent chunks of lobster, and it's absolutely mouth-watering."

"I love that you know me so well, Jorge."

And I hope that you still love me after this evening is over.

After placing our orders with the waitress, I was eager to hear how her evening had gone with Margo and Eva. She'd mentioned going with them to The Spicy Pineapple, which was a safe choice. After the fiasco there with Ria, her chances of showing her face again were pretty slim.

"It was so much fun! These past few weeks have been so busy, between work and, well, the whole Ria situation."

I didn't know how to reply because anything that came out of my mouth would eventually lead to us discussing a fake wedding. So, I shoved a piece of bread into my mouth.

"Anyway, they couldn't believe Ria just up and walked out of the restaurant! Talk about a drama queen."

I nodded while washing the bread down with some champagne, hoping Ginger would keep on talking, but she waited for me to respond. "That would be the understatement of the year."

Ginger told me all of the details regarding her promotion, and I found myself completely entranced by her beauty. She was wearing the diamond tennis bracelet on her left wrist, and it was impossible not to notice how all of the diamonds sparkled together with her engagement ring.

Fake engagement ring.

She started waving her hands in the air for emphasis, and fellow diners took notice of her jewelry. Several women eyed the engagement ring with envy while sitting across from their husbands and wearing ones considerably smaller. But Ginger wasn't the type of woman who cared about the size or cost of something.

All she cared about was authenticity, and I suddenly realized that life without Ginger would be meaningless. She let out a long moan while taking a bite of her lobster. "Jorge, you were right about the lobster. This is the best I've ever had."

"You deserve it after earning that promotion, Ginger. So,

did you say that you also get more vacation days? Because I'd love to visit Paris with you sometime."

As long as you don't kill me over what I'm about to ask of you.

Whenever I interacted with Ria—whether it was about work or something personal—she always came off as phony. Which oddly suited her well, given how plastic her body had become. The last time she discussed plastic surgery with me, she was looking into butt implants. I didn't want to offend her, so I merely nodded along. But nothing about her felt or looked real anymore.

Her personality aside, Ria was attractive before she went under the knife. Now she was a walking advertisement for silicone and collagen.

"Of course," Ginger said while continuing to speak, "as soon as they mentioned more vacation time, my first thought was 'where am I going to go?' But I'd love to go to Paris with you!"

I reached across the table and took her left hand, smiling at her while once again rubbing circles over the ring. There were a million things that I wanted to say to Ginger at that moment. I tried to pour my heart out to her and tell her that she had turned me into a better man. She needed to know before we started our relationship, I was nothing.

But that had to wait until Ria was out of the picture.

"There are plenty of places we can visit during your time off, but Paris is definitely at the top of my list. We should visit the Swiss Alps sometime too. I have a feeling you'd love it there."

Ginger smiled at me while leaning in for a kiss. "You are the most romantic man that I've ever known, Jorge Stein."

"Only because you've made me that way, Ginger Bowers."

As we resumed eating, I found it hard to look at anything other than her ring and the bogus symbol it represented. It was one big reminder that I had to throw a phony wedding ceremony and that Ginger needed to know about it sooner rather than later. But everything was going so well between us that night, that I couldn't find the right time to tell her.

Ginger caught me staring at it, though, and suddenly became insecure. "I should probably give this back to you, Jorge. I'm sorry for still wearing it."

I shifted in my seat, realizing that it was now or never. "Actually, I want you to keep it, Ginger."

Her face lit up as she clapped her hands together excitedly. "Wait, are you serious?"

Oh, God, no. She thinks that I'm about to propose! "Well, yes, you see—"

"Jorge, I can't believe you want me to keep this ring! Oh, God! I can't remember the last time I was so happy! Today feels like one big walking dream!"

Well, it's about to turn into one big walking nightmare.

Ginger started fanning her face as the tears fell down her cheeks, and I wanted nothing more than to slither under the table and disappear.

"You see, it's just that—"

"First, I get a promotion at the spa, and now this! Oh, I'm sorry, Jorge! I keep interrupting you." She smoothed the white napkin on her lap while composing herself, and at that point, everyone on the terrace was looking at us.

This cannot be happening to me.

I spent the next couple of minutes trying to find the words to tell Ginger about needing a fake wedding ceremony, but I couldn't speak. Not with so many people staring at us so intensely, and especially not after realizing Ginger was expecting a real marriage proposal.

Ginger couldn't take it any longer. "Jorge, please, just ask me! I can't wait any longer!"

"Ria emailed me the morning after we met her at The Spicy Pineapple for drinks."

Ginger's face instantly turned to ice. Her expression fell, and her shoulders slumped, and with it went my heart. "Why did she email you?"

"Because she still doesn't believe that you're my fiancée, and she's refusing to leave the company."

Ginger stood up as she leaned across the table. "Are you kidding me right now? How could she not believe us, Jorge? She got up and left after seeing the tennis bracelet you gave me!"

"Is everything all right over here?"

Ginger sat down while nodding at the waitress, who then looked at me with concern. "Yes, I'm terribly sorry."

Once the waitress left, I decided just to rip off the bandage. "Anyway, she'll never believe that I'm getting married and that I'll never be completely rid of her. Feeling incredibly frustrated, I called my friend Gavin who suggested that we follow through with a wedding ceremony."

Ginger leaned back in her chair, slumping as all color drained from her face. "That's why you told me to keep the engagement ring."

I hated that she said it as a statement, rather than posing it as a question. I reached across the table and began rubbing the ring again as I held her hand. "Ginger, you must know that I love you! I've never been in love with any other woman before you, and this isn't how I thought tonight would go. Not that I thought you'd necessarily be excited about being my fake bride, but certainly not this."

"Are you honestly going to throw an entire wedding ceremony just to get rid of this woman, Jorge? Because if you are, then maybe it's time you get your lawyers involved. I know you're terrified of ruining your reputation in the diamond business, but this is getting insane. It's one thing to be a fake fiancée, but I don't even know how I'd pull off being a fake bride."

It became incredibly uncomfortable between us over the next several minutes, which we spent shifting uncomfortably in our seats while poking away at our key lime pies.

"Well," I said, "I think I can create some fake marriage documents. At least the certificate, although I'm not sure what else is needed. I'll probably just hit up my lawyer, explain the situation, and see what he says."

"Or you could hit up your lawyer, tell him that Ria embezzled near a million dollars from the company, and let them handle the rest. She'll probably be forced out of the company while the investigation was going on, anyway, and I'd be more than happy to show them everything that I found."

I let out a deep sigh before trying one last time to convince her. "When I say that Ria could ruin my reputation, Ginger, I'd lose everything. I would be out of business within a matter of weeks, if not days." I reached across the table again, taking her hand and stroking it with my thumb. "All I'm asking is for you to get a wedding gown—on me, of course—while I work on the legal documents. Then we'll figure out our next steps."

Ginger's frustration was apparent as she thought about what I was asking of her before she finally nodded. "Fine, but if this doesn't do the trick, then your only other option is getting your lawyers involved. This ends my involvement in the whole fiasco, Jorge. If we have a fake wedding ceremony and Ria still doesn't leave you alone, don't ask me to help out anymore. Do you understand me?"

I silently nodded as we finished our dessert.

What have I done?

I walked her to her car, and when I kissed her, she wasn't nearly as passionate as usual. Her entire body had gone limp, too, and I realized that I'd ruined her otherwise enjoyable day.

"I am so, so sorry, Ginger. Do you want to come back to my place tonight?"

"No," she said while getting into her car. "I just need to go to bed. I'll call you tomorrow."

Ginger practically sped out of the parking lot, hightailing it onto the highway as people watched in horror. My driver held the door to my limousine open. I slid inside and closed my eyes the entire way home.

And as I made my way inside my penthouse, I couldn't help but wonder if I'd pushed Ginger too far this time.

17

Ginger

My day off should have been spent either sunbathing on the beach in my new blue bikini or shopping in downtown Miami. But there I was, smack dab in the middle of Natalia's Bridal Salon with Margo and Eva, doing a poor job at pretending to be excited over wedding dresses. Even the sales associate had a hard time believing that I was looking forward to getting married, and why wouldn't she? I was through with the whole Jorge and Ria scenario. If I weren't madly in love with him, I would have bailed on his ass the second Ria came into the picture.

It was just the three of us in the salon, which meant that we had their full attention. I would have preferred it if other women were in there, too, since it'd take some of the pressure off of me. Instead, several women walked past while peering their faces into the windows, ogling over all of the gorgeous gowns. I knew they saw me and my fake engagement ring, and were instantly jealous. They probably assumed that I was marrying a wealthy man and would never have to work again in my life.

How about we trade places, ladies?

The sales associate walked out of the back room with a breathtaking white gown saturated in designer crystals. It was a dress that I would have fawned over on any other occasion, such as leafing through bridal magazines on my lunch hour. I would also remind myself that I could never afford such a lavish gown, not to mention it was far too much to spend on one day.

Eva's eyes bugged out when she saw the gown, and then she screeched so loud I was sure the crystal chandelier above us would burst, thereby causing shards of glass to scatter all over the immaculate marble floor.

"Oh, Ginger! You would look like a movie star in this gown! Please try it on!"

The sales associate smiled at Margo, waiting for her opinion. Tears formed in Margo's eyes while sipping on expensive champagne. "I completely agree with Eva. Ginger, you have to try that one on. Even if you don't go with it, just put it on for fun! Oh, look at all the crystals!"

Get yourselves together, ladies. It's not even for a real wedding!

"Fine, we'll put that on the rack to try on." The sales associate winced at my lackluster, monotone voice while placing it on the rack. I didn't mean to be so curt, but it wasn't exactly my idea of a fun way to spend an afternoon.

As soon as she was out of sight, Margo addressed the elephant in the room. "Ginger, I know all of this is a ruse, but you should at least have some fun. Look at where we are! Do you realize how many women would love just to be allowed into this place?"

They had a point. The owner of the shop, Natalia, was from Italy and only catered to the elite. Several celebrities had gotten married in gowns that she had designed too. I'd caught Eva eyeing a number of them in gossip magazines at work.

You usually had to book an appointment months in advance, but the second I had dropped Jorge's name, she asked if I could come down that day.

"I guess so. It just seems like a waste of money for a dress that I'll probably never wear. I mean, look at this price tag, you guys!"

Eva's eyes bugged out when she saw the six-digits.

"Well, I'm sure you can wear it someplace else."

"Where else would I wear this dress, Eva? Grocery shopping?"

Margo chuckled while sipping her champagne, and Eva shrugged, realizing that I had a good point.

"I just can't believe that I'm going to so many lengths over some guy."

Margo tilted her head at me, seemingly confused all of a sudden. "But I thought you said that you were in love with Jorge, Ginger."

I am in love with him. That's the problem.

"Let's just get this thing over with. The less time I spend trying on wedding dresses that I'll never wear, the less I have to think about all of the hoops I'm jumping through for Jorge and a wedding that isn't real."

Eva set down her champagne glass, walked over to me, and took both of my hands. "Ginger, I've never seen you this happy. Obviously not at this moment, but in general. Try not to be so upset at Jorge. He might be asking a lot of you, but it's only because he loves you."

Margo put her hand on my shoulder. "Eva's right, Ginger. Chase is always telling me how much Jorge has changed for the better. You two are meant to be together. So let's pick out an expensive wedding dress, and then use his credit card for a bite to eat afterward."

"Now, I'm starting to feel better," I said while smiling at them. "But only because we're going to eat after this and Jorge is paying."

After the sales associate put another few dresses on the rack for me to try, I went into the dressing room, donning each one. The first few didn't suit my figure at all, and the next two weren't nearly as pretty on me as they were on the rack. But the final dress, a stunning, cream-colored satin number with a long, floral train seemed to be the winner.

As I stared at myself in the mirror, the sales associate kept looking at my jewelry. "That ring and tennis bracelet are gorgeous."

"Thank you," I said while admiring both of them. "All of my jewelry is from my fiancée."

She clicked her tongue while straightening out my train. "He's obviously a keeper because I can tell that neither of those has fake stones. Good for you."

I smiled while admiring both the ring and bracelet and how they glistened from the light beaming off the chandelier.

"Her fiancée is a diamond broker," Eva said while pouring herself another glass of champagne.

I shot her a dirty look, begging her not to talk any more than absolutely necessary, especially since she was hitting the complimentary champagne pretty hard and hadn't eaten that day.

The sales associate's mouth fell open. "Oh, my. No wonder Natalia told us to take extra good care of you." For a woman who worked at a bridal salon and seemed to know a lot about diamonds, her hands sure were bare.

"That was sweet of her. So, what about you?"

She waved while admiring the dress on me. "I gave up on love a long time ago, which is odd, seeing how I work for a bridal designer. But I just love everything that has to do with weddings."

I knew Eva would chime in with her thoughts about love.

"It's hard finding the right guy, but everybody has a soulmate. You just have to keep putting yourself out there."

"She's right," Margo said. "I found mine with Chase, and we had a pretty rocky start. If I gave up every time I wanted to, then I wouldn't be happily married with a baby."

All three of them turned toward me as I continued standing in front of the mirror. I knew what the ladies were waiting for me to say. They wanted me to tell them that Jorge was my soulmate. But if he and I were destined to be together, then why was I having to go to such great lengths to be with him?

"The dating scene can be rough," I finally said, "but if you let your intuition be your navigation system, then you'll survive." It might have been one of the corniest things I'd ever said, but it was all I could come up with.

Until Ria was finally out of the picture, I refused to believe that Jorge was my soulmate. I would only be setting myself up for disappointment.

Once the sales associate was out of sight again, I slipped out of the dress and threw another few into the dressing room. Even though it was for a fake wedding, I wanted to make sure that I picked out the best dress. I wanted Ria's eyes to pop out of her silicone face when she saw me wearing the most elaborate gown in Miami. Because once that fake wedding ceremony was over, I would make sure that she never came between Jorge and me ever again.

Two hours, three bottles of champagne, and dozens of dresses later, all of us were officially exhausted and in dire need of some food. Eva had worked up a significant buzz and was in urgent need of something to soak it all up, while Margo looked like she could fall asleep at any moment. Our sales associate had given us some space, and as I stood there, looking at myself in the mirror, Margo piped up.

"I know we told you to have some fun with this whole thing, but aren't you a little too invested in this bridal gown?"

"Yeah," Eva said. "I think that one from two hours ago, with the crystals, is what you should get."

I reached for it on the rack, held it up to my body, and nodded.

"Sold. All right, let's get out of here. I'm about to faint from lack of food."

The sales associate's eyes lit up when Jorge's credit card was instantly approved, and I knew what she was thinking: gold digger. Sure, she had been courteous and treated us with nothing but respect, but I would think the same thing in her position. It wasn't like I had acted even remotely excited about the process, so I was sure—from an outsider's perspective—that I came across as shallow.

I considered taking the wedding dress home first, but all of our stomachs were grumbling so loud that I knew it wasn't an option. So, I hung it in the backseat of my car, deciding that we'd ask for a table outside. That way, I could keep an eye on it, especially since it was impossible to hang it without exposing the price tag.

We pulled into the parking lot of Seafood Divine, the same restaurant that Jorge had taken me to the other night.

"They have the best cheddar-stuffed lobster here, you guys."

Eva ran her hand up and down her stomach. "I'm just gonna stuff my face with biscuits until the food comes."

"You and me both," Margo said as we made our way into

the restaurant…and stopped dead in our tracks by the sight of Ria coming out.

She took one look at me and smirked. "Ginger, what an interesting surprise. Seafood Divine isn't an easy place to get a table, and you usually need to drop a name just to get a seat. And it looks like it's just you girls. Well, maybe they'll—"

Ria stopped talking as her eyes landed on the wedding dress. Her high heels clicked along the pavement as she made her way over to it, obnoxiously pressing her face against the window to see the price tag and designer name.

I was not in the mood for her games. "Can I help you with something, Ria? Or do you make it a habit to look into everyone's car?"

She turned back to us, pulling her sunglasses off and glaring into my eyes. "You're really marrying Jorge, aren't you?"

"Of course, I am, Ria. I don't know why you'd ever doubt that in the first place."

She looked at Eva, who was standing next to me with her arms folded across her chest.

"I'm Eva, her maid of honor."

Margo stood on the other side of me, also with her hands folded across her chest. "And I'm Margo, one of her bridesmaids."

Ria's face instantly went pale as she was overcome with shock. She started shaking her head while tears streamed down her face. Usually, I'd reach out to a crying woman, even ones I didn't know, but this bitch had it coming.

"Why else would I spend money on a wedding dress if I weren't getting married, Ria? You saw how expensive it was. Even Jorge wouldn't blow that kind of money away for something that wasn't real." My heart was beating a mile a minute, but I somehow found a way to remain calm on the outside.

I've never been good at lying.

"I can't believe that I've wasted the best years of my life on that jerk! Good luck with that rat bastard, Ginger! I hope he treats you better than he's treated me!"

All three of us watched as she rushed over to her car and sped off.

"Did I just convince Ria that Jorge and I were *actually* getting married?"

Margo and Eva gave each other high-fives, while I stood there motionless, shocked that I had inadvertently found a way to get Ria out of our life.

"I'd say so," Margo replied. "Now, let's go celebrate with some seafood. I'm wearing my stretchy pants today."

18

Jorge

My employees were busy working from my downtown office, scurrying back and forth while holding documents. I watched them from behind the glass door to my office, my hands shoved deep into my pockets while waiting for Barry Livingston to answer me. Everyone seemed engrossed in their work, completely unaware that I was on a conference call with my lawyer, asking how hard it would be to create a fake marriage license.

I had Googled how to do it myself, but it was too much of a risk. Ria might have been a condescending, ruthless woman, but she was smart as hell. It was one of the reasons I'd gone into business with her in the first place.

After pounding away on his keyboard for several awkward

minutes, Barry finally spoke up. "Look, Jorge, obviously I can show you how to make a passable document. Hell, I could create a believable one in less than an hour. But you're asking me to do something that could cause me to lose my license."

I knew this shit would happen.

"Obviously, I would never do that to you, Barry. All I'm asking is to show me how, and I'll do everything on my end. Nobody will suspect a thing, not to mention the fact that nothing will come of it. Ginger and I aren't trying to screw the government over by pretending to be married. As soon as Ria sees it and she's out of my life, I'll chuck it right into a burning fire."

"Well, you've seen a marriage certificate before, right Jorge? Just copy something you find online. Ria won't know the difference."

I closed my eyes while shaking my head. "We're talking about a woman who flew all the way to Miami because she wasn't convinced that I was engaged. This is the same woman, mind you, who still doesn't believe it after seeing the engagement ring for herself. If I show her a fake marriage license, she'll laugh, and then I'll never get rid of her!"

Barry typed some more, and I wondered what the hell he was even doing. He wasn't a lawyer who specialized in divorces, but he had handled several of them over the years. He could spot any fake document within seconds, and that was one of the reasons I kept him on retainer.

"I get it, Jorge. You want it to be believable. The problem is that if this ever got traced back to me, the legal system would have a field day with my showing someone how to forge legal documents."

With all of the money that I give you, can't you do me this one favor?

"Rest assured, Barry, that I would never let that happen to you. The only place this is going to be seen is between Ria, Ginger, and myself. There's no legal reason for Ria to take this to a courthouse to have it verified, either. Especially—"

I paused, realizing that I didn't want Barry to know about the embezzlement. If he found out, then I'd have to move forward with charges, and Ria would ruin my reputation somehow.

"Especially what, Jorge?"

"Never mind, I was going off on a tangent. Anyway, as you can see, I'm in quite the bind right now."

He obnoxiously exhaled, causing me to roll my eyes yet again. "I just don't understand why you're going to such great lengths to get rid of a woman, Jorge. I mean, I've dealt with difficult females over the years, but this is insane. What could she have possibly done that has you shaking in your shoes? You've never been that kind of a man."

Oh, she only embezzled about a million bucks out of this company...That's all.

"You know how women are, Barry. She's one of those psychotic, clingy types who won't leave you alone without solid proof that you're not interested. Ria could physically see my erection go limp just by looking at her, and she'd still find a way to try to stay in my life."

"Yep, I've been there, my friend. I made the mistake of having an affair, and my side piece wouldn't leave me alone. She kept texting and calling me at all hours of the night, begging me to leave my family for her. Until she saw me out to dinner with my wife and kids one night. Once she noticed how happy I was, that was all it took for her to stop contacting me. Something clicked in her head. So believe me, I get it. And I've been faithful to my wife ever since."

I instantly thought about all of the evenings I'd spent with Ginger, stealing kisses over dinner while gazing into each other's eyes. Not once did I ever want to do that with Ria. "I only wish it were that easy with Ria. Ginger and I were all over each other at The Spicy Pineapple, and I thought she bought it after storming out of the place. But sure enough, I woke up to a nasty email from her the next morning. Anyway, I'll make it up to you however you'd like, Barry."

"Are you going to put on a wedding ceremony too? With pictures and all?"

My mind started racing as I thought about how that would even happen. We'd have to invite enough people to make it look real, but not so many that word got out it was all a hoax.

This is a nightmare.

"I haven't thought that far ahead yet, Barry. But I gave—"

Ria suddenly barged into my office, which I'd forgotten to lock, with tears in her eyes. I stood in front of my desk so she wouldn't see that I had my speakerphone on. Whatever she had to say, I wanted my lawyer to hear. Screw worrying about my reputation being ruined by this woman. I needed her out of my life ASAP.

"You son of a bitch! Do you know how much time I wasted on you? Get your checkbook out, mister, because I want a lot more than your original offer! If you think that a measly half a billion dollars is enough to keep me from ruining your reputation, then you've got another think coming!"

I cleared my throat while adjusting my tie, but she spoke again before I could say anything.

"I saw Ginger at Seafood Divine with a wedding dress hanging in her car. How is it that I can give you the best damn sex of your life and that bitch gets a million-dollar engagement ring, a diamond tennis bracelet, and a six-figure dress that only someone with my body could pull off?" She pointed to her breast implants, which I found utterly repulsive, then continued ranting. "I just can't believe that you wifed her up so fast! You two were speaking on the phone for a year, and then within a month of coming home, you're engaged! Who does that sort of thing?"

I shrugged while smiling at her, realizing that the tables had finally turned. "What else can I say, Ria? When you know, you know."

Before continuing her rant, she patted her hair while quickly checking herself in the mirror hanging on the wall. "And yes, I took just under a million dollars from this company, Jorge. Do you know why? Because I never got as much money as I deserved! You have always gotten the bigger checks, even though we did the same amount of work." Ria rubbed her knees. "Although, I did a hell of a lot more physical work if you know what I mean."

"Please don't remind me."

"Whatever, you jerk. You know that Ginger bitch will never be as good as me. Oh, and good luck with this stupid-ass company because you're gonna need it once I'm gone. Do you realize how hard your job is about to become? You can't just let anyone else slide into my position, Jorge. Oh, and your precious reputation in the diamond community is about to be ruined if you don't double your original offer!"

I swallowed a huge lump in my throat as she got closer to my face. She came within a few inches, daring me to speak. But I knew better, and that pissed her off.

"Well, aren't you going to say anything, jerk-wad?"

My lawyer loudly cleared his throat after several minutes of silence. "This is Barry Livingston, Mr. Stein's attorney. If I understood you correctly, ma'am, you just admitted to embezzlement. Is that correct?"

I slowly stepped aside, and Ria's eyes landed on the red light on my speakerphone.

Ria kept looking between me and the speakerphone, trying to find the words to say. Her tongue repeatedly licked her lips, too, as though preparing for a speech. But there was nothing else she could say. She bolted out of my office, nearly hitting her head on the door on the way out.

"Did you catch all of that, Barry?"

He chuckled while typing away at his keyboard. "Oh, yeah.

Plus, all of our calls are recorded. We'll take care of everything. By the way, do you still need that marriage license?"

I leaned back in my chair, a huge smile forming on my face as I rested my feet on the desk. "Nope."

I breathed a massive sigh of relief as I relaxed for a few minutes, surprised that I'd finally gotten rid of Ria. Now that I didn't need to forge any documents, I could focus on my real job.

Except all I could think about was celebrating with Ginger.

So, I quickly scanned my emails before leaving the office. The only one that seemed somewhat important was from the De Veers Diamond Group, but it appeared to just be a follow-up email. Nothing in the header suggested that I should be alarmed.

On my way out of the building, I stopped at my secretary's desk. "I might be out next week. Please only contact me for anything that can't wait until I return."

She nodded, and I was so thankful to have a trustworthy assistant.

As soon as I got into my car, I called Ginger to tell her the good news.

"Jorge, you'll never believe what happened to us today!"

"No, Ginger. You'll never believe what happened to me today!"

19

Ginger

When Jorge invited me out for drinks at The Spicy Pineapple that night, the only thing he said was that we would be celebrating. I assumed it had something to do with Ria leaving for Belgium, and while I never even wanted to speak or hear her name ever again, I gladly accepted his invitation. The past few weeks had been an emotional rollercoaster. And as much as I would have loved for it to have just been the two of us, I was elated to see our friends waiting for us at a large booth.

Margo, Chase, and Eva were laughing and enjoying some appetizers by the time we sat down.

"Oh, this is wonderful! I didn't know all of you guys would be here!"

Chase wrapped his arm around Margo, kissing her on her forehead at the same time. "How could I not celebrate with you two. I've only been telling Jorge to ditch Ria since the second he met her. Besides, Margo and I will use any excuse to get out of the house nowadays."

Margo quickly pulled out her cellphone. "That reminds me. Our babysitter hasn't texted us to let us know everything's okay yet."

"Relax," Chase said while chuckling. "We haven't even been gone an hour yet. I can't wait to see how you act once she starts school."

As Jorge wrapped his arm around me, it was impossible to ignore how uncomfortable Eva suddenly felt. She was the only one there without a partner. And out of all of us, she was someone who thrived on being in a relationship.

Eva shifted in her seat and decided to break the sudden tension. "So, tell us exactly what happened when Ria showed up at your office, Jorge."

I looked up at Jorge, who immediately smiled upon remembering the whole situation.

Yes, please tell them how she dug her own grave.

"I was on the phone with my lawyer, asking him how to create a marriage certificate without legally filing it when she came barging into my office. I stood in front of the phone so she wouldn't see the red light on the speaker, and my lawyer knew better than to say a word. And then Ria admitted to everything. She laid into me about wasting her time, then confessed to embezzling nearly a million bucks."

All of us at the table burst out laughing before he kept talking.

"Anyway, I was too stunned to say anything back to her. And she just kept staring at me. When she finally asked why I was so quiet, I moved aside, and that's when my lawyer started speaking. She bolted out of the office so fast that she nearly hit her head on the door!"

I wish she'd knocked herself out on that door!

Chase's eyes went to my engagement ring, which I had completely forgotten to take off. "So, now that Ria's out of the picture, how much longer will you be wearing that diamond, Ginger? Or is it no longer a 'fake,' if you catch my drift?"

Jorge shifted uncomfortably in his seat a little bit, but I prevented myself from getting too excited. I probably should have taken it off, but I loved how people automatically looked at it. I had never been the focus of envy before, and it felt amazing.

But I also wanted to be the focus of real envy.

If and when he does propose, it's not going to be in front of a bunch of people. Calm down, woman!

Just as he was about to speak, Guadalupe and Yuslan showed up and pulled up a few chairs. Before they could see the ring, however, I quickly slipped it off and tucked it into my purse. I would never hear the end of it if Guadalupe saw that thing on my finger.

"All of my girls are here," she yelled enthusiastically while sitting down. "Oh, this is wonderful, especially after the day that I had. I'll tell you girls something, as much as I love owning a spa, some of our clients are a little too uppity. Several women came in and acted as though I should have rolled out the red carpet."

Margo, Eva, and I chuckled while nodding.

"That's what happens when you cater to the elite," I reminded her. "It's a wonderful place to work, but some of the clients definitely want you to treat them like royalty."

Eva snickered. "Yeah, and most of them are just married to rich guys without ever having worked a day in their life." It was unusual to see Eva so cynical.

"Eva, I'm loving your newfound cynicism."

"That's what happens when you stay single for so long."

And just like that, the air at the table got tense and quiet.

Yuslan smiled while leaning back in his chair. "What are we drinking tonight?"

I took a long sip of my drink while smiling at him. "All of us are having their spicy pineapple margaritas. You two should try one, too. So good!"

Guadalupe leaned across the table to get a better look at Jorge. "You know, Jorge, Ginger is one of our best employees. She never needs any help when it comes to doing her job, and I have yet to find any errors in her work. She's also one of the sweetest, most giving women I've ever met."

Yuslan nodded approvingly while sipping his margarita, wincing at how spicy it was. "My wife is right, Jorge. She's a good woman who deserves a good man."

"Believe me, I have every intention of treating her like the queen that she is, and I don't have any plans on leaving Miami. This is my home, and I know that Ginger feels the same way."

Our eyes met as he nuzzled my nose, and I realized that nothing could ruin our night.

"Get a room, you two," Eva said while drinking another spicy pineapple margarita. "I'm sorry, it's just kind of weird being the only one without a date tonight."

Guadalupe leaned back and scoured the restaurant. "Eva, I'm going to find you an alto, oscuro y guapo man tonight!"

She held her hands up while shaking her head profusely. "No, please don't do that, Guadalupe. Thank you for being so nice, but I was just joking around."

Margo and I burst out laughing because we completely understood Eva's apprehension. Guadalupe wouldn't have thought twice about approaching a man and telling him that he should date Eva, and that's not how Eva wanted to meet her next boyfriend.

"All right," Guadalupe said while facing the table again. "But you're going to find a good man one of these days, mark my words!"

I rested a little bit more against Jorge, enjoying the sound of his heart beating.

"I miss working with you guys," Margo said. "Especially now that Ginger has been promoted and Eva has her old job back."

Chase smiled at her while brushing some hair out of her

face. "I can easily take care of Joanna if you want to go back to work. Besides, I love working from home."

Margo burst out laughing while shaking her head at him. "Are you crazy? I can barely keep up with her as it is, and as she gets older, it'll only get harder. I'll go back in due time."

Guadalupe looked so happy, smiling at all of us at the table. It was as though we were one big family.

Yuslan tapped Jorge on the shoulder. "Jorge, would you mind sitting with me at the bar for a few minutes?"

"Sure, no problem."

The two of them sat down at the bar behind us, and I couldn't help but lean back in my seat, wanting to listen in on their conversation.

"Two spicy pineapple margaritas," Yuslan said. "I've noticed a change in you lately, Jorge. You seem happier. Is it because Ria's gone?"

"That certainly adds to it, but most of it has to do with Ginger."

I casually turned around to see Yuslan smiling at him. "I figured as much. I went through a similar change after meeting Guadalupe many, many years ago."

Jorge chuckled while sipping his drink. "I'd love to hear about it."

"I dated so many women before her, Jorge. Dozens of them would flock to me because, according to Guadalupe, I was alto, oscuro y guapo. As you can see, that's changed over time."

"Oh, stop, Yuslan. You're still a good-looking guy."

Yuslan shook his head while chuckling. "Not like I used to be. The women would pounce on me the second I walked into any public place. I was like a magnet for them, you see. And then I met Guadalupe, and everything changed."

"How did you know she was the one?"

Yuslan looked off into the distance. "She was different than the rest. Sure, she made it clear that she found me physically attractive. But she wouldn't put up with my flirting with other women. Before her, I wouldn't think twice about hitting on women in front of each other."

"That's how you knew?"

"Well, that and something else, Jorge. I knew she was the one because whenever I wasn't with her, I felt incomplete. A man should be able to stand on his own two feet. He should be able to make his way in the world without any help, and if you do it right, you'll attract an equally strong woman to have by your side. And that's how I felt about Guadalupe."

Jorge nodded while sipping his drink, taking in Yuslan's wisdom. "That's how I'm starting to feel about Ginger. I felt terrible about asking her to help out with the Ria situation, but I also knew that she could pull it off. She's the strongest, most independent woman that I've ever known. And I can tell that if I lost all of my money tomorrow, she'd still want to be with me."

Yuslan patted him on the back while standing up. "That's how you know, Jorge. And I could have told you that Ginger wasn't the materialistic type a long time ago. Now let's go back and join our strong, independent women at the table."

I quickly sat up in my seat, not wanting it to be evident that I'd been eavesdropping on their conversation.

Jorge smirked at me as he sat down. "Well, now that we're all here and liquored up, I'd like to discuss going away with Ginger for a week."

My eyes instantly lit up. "Oh, Jorge! I'd love to go on vacation. Where to, though?"

"I thought that we could celebrate your recent promotion at a spa in Paris. What do you say?"

I started fanning my face, just as I'd done at Seafood Divine when I thought he was going to propose to me. Right as I was about to answer him, Eva spoke up.

"Are you kidding me? Ginger, you have to go to Paris! It's the most romantic city in the world! You two can kiss in front of the Eiffel Tower, feed each other chocolate-covered strawberries in a Parisian cafe, and walk on The Ponts des Arts!"

Margo nearly choked on her margarita. "The what des what, Eva?"

Eva clasped her hands together while looking up at the ceiling, pretending it was the Parisian night sky. "The Ponts des Arts, Margo! You and Jorge inscribe your initials on a padlock, click it onto the metal, and then throw the key into the water!"

"I hate to break it to you," Jorge said, "but the government put a stop to it in 2015. All of the locks are gone, and they even inserted panels to prevent it from happening anymore."

Eva could not have been more devastated, but she made herself feel better by downing her third margarita.

"Well," I said, "as much as I'd love to go to Paris right now, I don't have vacation time for five more months."

Guadalupe leaned back in her chair and folded her arms. "Ginger, I thought you knew me better than that. Of course you can go to Paris with Jorge!"

"Are you sure, Guadalupe? I mean, we just got the new computer software installed, and I don't want to go against the rules."

"I make the rules," Guadalupe replied, "and I'm ordering you to spend a week in Paris with your alto, oscuro y guapo man!"

20

Jorge
One Week Later

Spending a week in Paris with Ginger was nothing short of amazing. We made love every night in our five-star hotel, ate at some of the best restaurants, and even saw a few plays. Leaving the most romantic city in the world had been bittersweet, though. On the one hand, we would be returning to Miami without worrying about Ria coming between us. But on the other hand, both of us knew that work had piled up while we were away.

Ginger and I had showered together that morning and discussed working from home just so we could spend more time together. But we knew there would be physical mail waiting for us at work.

It was business as usual as I walked into my Miami office that Monday morning. My first order of the day was finding someone to fill Ria's position. Ginger and I had discussed my options for replacing her while in Paris, and she agreed that my secretary would be the right candidate. She'd been with me from day one and needed little to no guidance on how to do her job. In her spare time, she had taken it upon herself to learn everything there was to know about the diamond industry. But the most important qualification was that she was trustworthy.

Of course, to be fair, I'd officially have to list the position opening and interview other candidates. The position would come with a significant pay increase and better stock options, which meant that giving it to my secretary would undoubtedly result in people complaining behind her back. They'd also speculate that she had slept her way to the top, too.

That's what was going through my mind as I picked up a stack of documents from my lawyer, thankful that I'd decided to come into work that day.

They were waiting for me on my desk first thing that morning. As I scoured through all of the papers, I was blown away at how badly Ria had screwed me over. It wasn't just the nearly one million dollars that she embezzled from the company. She also messed with our company's investments, for reasons that were still unknown, which caused me to lose a large amount of money in the stock market.

According to the documents, Ria had cashed out one of our major investments, redistributed the funds into lower-yielding bonds, and some of the money from the investment sale was unaccounted for. It was bad enough that she had embezzled our regular income but messing with our investment portfolio had a worse impact on the company's long-term goals. Whoever took over her job would have to sit down and run some serious numbers before the company could move forward.

In other words, I didn't have time for this bullshit.

My secretary knocked on my door right as I was eager for a break.

"Come on in."

She shut the door behind her while holding a letter in her hand. I thought I noticed a "certified" stamp on it.

As she went to put it on my desk, I realized that I was in desperate need of a distraction for a few minutes. "I know that you respect my privacy, but aren't you going to ask about my trip to Paris?"

"Of course, Mr. Stein. I know that things were quite tense in the office right before you left, due to Ria, so I hope you enjoyed your vacation. I assume you and Ginger had fun in France?"

"It was amazing, and you need to put it on your bucket list. We saw a handful of plays. However, they weren't nearly as good as those on Broadway. I was amazed at how fulfilling a simple French pastry and coffee could be for breakfast, too. Of course, it probably helped that we were in Paris. The ones you can buy at the store here aren't nearly as good as we had.

Hell, who am I kidding? I never let myself eat that kind of food."

All she did was smile at me, while awkwardly shifting back and forth in her shoes. Typically she was a bit more talkative, but I got a distinct feeling that she was hiding something.

"That sounds wonderful, Mr. Stein." Something was definitely off with her that morning.

"Is everything all right? You look...worried. Did something happen while I was gone? Ria didn't come back here, did she?" I stood up from my desk, suddenly worried that Ria had, in fact, shown back up at our office.

She shook her head at me, causing me to breathe a sigh of relief. "No, Mr. Stein. But I had to sign for a certified letter on Friday from the De Veers Diamond Group. I was going to call or text you about it, but I didn't want to ruin your vacation with Ginger. After everything that happened with Ria, I'm sure you were eager to get away."

I practically yanked the letter out of her hand, causing her to recoil in fear. "The De Veers Diamond Group never sends me certified mail."

"I'm so sorry, Mr. Stein. I should have called you right away, but I figured you'd be back in a few days anyway."

Yes, you most certainly should have contacted me right away.

With a wave of my hand, I dismissed her from my office and read it to myself.

There was a miner's strike at the diamond mine that I owned in Africa. It was the same one that had been striking off and on over the past few weeks, only returning to work every time Ria or I authorized a small wage increase. Their new demands were too complicated for me to spend time working on, and this was Ria's department. She handled payroll and everything related to human resources.

I ran my hand through my hair, realizing that I was in way over my head. This wasn't something that I could handle on my own, and the longer it waited, the more money I stood to lose.

And that's when I remembered the email they had sent me right before I went to Paris with Ginger. I pulled it up on my laptop and read it over.

Mr. Stein,

The miners are getting ready to protest yet again. They are not happy with the small, minuscule pay raises your company has given them. They've also expressed concern over their working conditions and benefits packages.

If you meet their demands within five business days, they will not strike.

If you do not meet their demands within five business days, they will strike until you or someone from your company comes to Africa to meet with them.

Sincerely,

De Veers Diamond Group

Son of a bitch! Who the hell would I send to Africa?

If I'd read that email before leaving for Paris with Ginger, I would have immediately authorized whatever the hell they wanted, because frankly, I was getting tired of dealing with this issue. Of course, I supported fair wages and decent working conditions, but there was no way I could go to Africa myself.

This is why I have avoided romantic relationships all of my life. All they do is get in the way of work.

I shook my head, refusing to allow myself to feel that way about Ginger. I was a changed man, and life without her wouldn't be worth living. This was just another hoop for us to get through, and after our trip to Paris, we felt more durable than ever.

Especially with Ria out of the picture.

I let out a long sigh, then got to work on finding a replacement.

As I was typing up a job posting, I found myself becoming angrier. I owned the damn company, and it would have been so easy just to hand it over to my secretary, along with her new title. She was single, too, and didn't have any children. So going to Africa for who knows how long would have been a breeze. I kept looking up at her through my glass doors, watching her work on the computer.

She was so damn efficient and knew what the hell she was doing.

But just knowing that she sat on this all weekend got under my skin. The woman had been working for me for years, and she knew damn well that anything from De Veers was considered urgent. She also knew that Ria handled everything with De Veers and that she was no longer with the company.

If only she'd called me!

Once I finished typing up the job posting, my next business order was going over every employee profile to find a suitable candidate. That took me the rest of the day since my company was so damn big. But as I flipped through every profile, I realized that I no longer trusted anyone to do Ria's job. She had done so much damage to me, both professionally and emotionally. Anyone I hired would be too much of a risk. But if I didn't hire someone right away, I could lose everything I had worked so hard for all at once.

Then I turned my attention to the dire situation with the miners and composed my email.

De Veers Diamond Group:

I received your certified letter this morning after I returned from a short vacation. To say that I'm shocked at the miner's strike would be an understatement, but rest assured that I will resolve this issue immediately. Please reassure them that I wholeheartedly support paying them a livable wage, along with providing safe working conditions.

However, the person who handled human resources and anything related to the payroll is no longer with my company. I'm searching for a replacement for this position, but in the meantime, I want to address this right away.

In regard to this being handled in Africa, I am asking for some leeway. Between having to hire someone new to manage this and just returning from a trip myself, I do not see how I'm able to send someone down to Africa.

Can we please find a way to resolve this remotely?

Sincerely,

Jorge Stein

Within minutes of sending the email, they replied back.

Mr. Stein,

Thank you for reaching out to us. Unfortunately, this must be addressed in person at this point. The miners want to speak with a representative from your company directly.

Please let us know when this can be arranged.

Sincerely,

De Veers Diamond Group

I slammed my laptop shut so hard that my secretary jumped out of her chair.

Looks like I'm back to square one because God forbid anything goes right in my life.

21

Ginger

There were fewer things that I enjoyed more than sipping coffee on my small balcony, which overlooked the gorgeous, crystal-clear ocean. Ever since I had moved into my condo, I had spent nearly every morning watching the waves crash against the shore while sipping Cuban coffee. But as much as I loved my condo and the view, I was starting to yearn for something bigger.

There were a few other condos in the development that were much larger, and naturally, they came with bigger price tags. I had considered moving into one since it would give me three bedrooms instead of two. Right now, I had my own home office and a bedroom, but it would be nice to have a guest room. Many of my high school and college friends had left Miami, and I would have loved to have a place for them to stay whenever they visited.

But my parents instilled in me the value of money, and I knew just how wasteful paying rent could be.

After pouring myself another cup of coffee, I headed into my home office and reviewed my five-year plan. It was something that I'd been putting off ever since Jorge and I had become more than friends, and if he had proposed to me in Paris, then I would have put it off some more, but that had never happened. I had thought he would have done so after one of the plays or on one of our several moonlight walks, but he never did. By the time we got back to the states, even though I was still very happy with him, I realized that I still wanted to move forward with my life.

And hopefully, in due time, he would ask me to marry him.

Relax, Ginger. You just started dating him.

As I looked over my monthly budget, I decided that I could afford a house within one to two years with my raise. I would double my monthly payments toward my student loans and deposits into my savings accounts, invest a little more money in the stock market, and could easily come up with a twenty percent down payment. It wouldn't be enough for a large, elaborate home, though. Just something to call my own while waiting on Jorge.

It wasn't what I thought would happen, though. I'd always assumed that once I graduated from college, I'd meet someone, fall in love, get engaged, and then buy a house with him.

But I knew he'd need some time to come down after ending things with Ria. Men tended to be much more cautious than women when it came to tying the knot. It still bothered me that life was turning out differently than I had planned.

After all, you were supposed to buy a house and get married right after college.

But I hated wasting money, and there was no point in paying rent when I could be investing it in a house, especially after seeing some of the new properties for sale. I could easily put down twenty percent within two years, as long as I committed to an investing schedule and stopped throwing money away on rent.

As I typed away, however, my eyes kept gravitating toward the engagement ring that I still wore despite us not being engaged.

Dozens of people had congratulated Jorge and me on our recent engagement in Paris, but instead of correcting them, Jorge thought it'd be fun to play along. That only got my hopes up, though. He came up with a proposal story that melted my heart, and each time he told it, I wanted to beg him just to do it already. The tension between us was too strong, anyway. It was clear that both of us wanted to be together, and Jorge had yet to ask for the ring back.

As I was tinkering with applying for a first-time homebuyer's savings account, Eva showed up with iced coconut lattes.

"I figured you could use some caffeine on your day off."

"I just downed my second cup of coffee, but I'll never turn down anything that tastes like coconut."

Eva looked over my shoulders to see what was on my computer. "Why are you looking at houses?"

I twirled the large diamond around my finger while looking at a stunning, ranch-style home not far away from where I was living. "With my raise at the spa, I'll be able to pay off my student loans in almost half the time. And after reviewing my budget today, I've decided to increase my monthly savings so I can buy a house in one to two years."

Eva sat down across from my desk, and I knew what she'd say before she even opened her mouth. "I know that you're on this independent-woman kick, but shouldn't you wait and see what happens with Jorge? I mean, the guy could probably buy the state of Florida. Why spend any of your money on a down payment for a house?"

"That's not the point, Eva. Who knows if and when Jorge will ever propose, and why should I keep paying rent? Besides, it's always good to plan ahead."

Eva lifted my left hand. "If he isn't going to propose, Ginger, then why hasn't he taken this ring back yet?"

"Because he knows how much I like it, Eva. As much as I love Jorge, I've learned that you should never assume things will work out with a guy."

"So, what if you buy a house, and then you guys get married?"

I shrugged while adding a few listings to my favorites. "Well, I could always sell it or rent it out to someone."

"Yeah, because if you marry Jorge, you'll really be hurting for money."

"You still don't get it, Eva. Until Jorge and I get married, I have to focus on myself. I know better than to depend on a man even though down deep inside I want to."

Eva shrugged again while taking a sip of her latte. "I just think it'd be a tad emasculating for you to buy a house while dating Jorge, that's all."

I folded my hands while leaning back in my chair. "Eva, Jorge doesn't need to worry about being emasculated. Believe me. He's all man underneath his clothing. And I bet he'd view it as a wise decision on my part. You're reading too much into this. Enough about me, all right. What's new with you?"

As Eva told me about having a crush on one of our male clients at the spa, I clicked away on different homes. Many of them were far outside of my price range, but there were quite a few that I could see myself living in. Of course, nothing within my budget was right on the water. If I ever wanted that view, I'd have to marry someone incredibly wealthy.

Jorge is incredibly wealthy, and you're still wearing the ring he gave you.

"Anyway," Eva continued, "he comes in all of the time for facials, and yesterday he got an hour-long massage. Ugh, I should have gone to school to become a masseuse. I'd give anything to rub my hands up and down his gorgeous body."

"I think Guadalupe and Yuslan have an education assistance program. They'll probably pay your tuition if you want to go back to school."

Eva shook her head while giggling. "Nah, I wouldn't want

to be on my feet all day. Well, I should get going. Let me know how the house-hunting turns out."

I laughed while watching her leave my condo. And just as I was about to shut my laptop down for the day, Jorge called me.

"Good morning, sweetie. How's work going?"

"Not that great. Are you sitting down?"

My heart sank as I sat down in my office chair.

"I am now. What's wrong?"

"I have to go to Africa."

"*What?* Why the hell are you going to Africa?" I could hear the frustration in his voice as he explained everything to me.

"Before we went to Paris, the De Veers Diamond Group sent me an email that I foolishly ignored. The miners are demanding huge changes to their income and benefits, and because I didn't respond within five days, they're now on strike."

I started pacing back and forth in my living room, my hands shaking with anger. "I don't understand, Jorge. Everything is done remotely nowadays, so why the hell do you have to go down there?"

"It's complicated, Ginger, and the worst part is that I don't know how long I'll be gone."

I fought the tears as they started to buildup in my eyes. *Don't you dare cry over a guy!* "So, you could be gone for a month? Or two months? Or a year? Is that what you're telling me, Jorge?"

"Please don't be so upset, Ginger, and I doubt it'll be a year."

"I hate to be *that* woman, but did you take me into consideration when you planned this trip?"

"Of course I did," he explained into the phone. "But Ginger, I don't have a choice. This would have been something that Ria handled, and now that she's gone, I have to do it myself."

"If Ria handled it, then why can't you just hire someone else for her position and send them down to deal with the problems on the other side of the world?"

"Because after what she did to the company, I don't know how I could trust anyone to do her job ever again, Ginger. Remember how we discussed having my secretary fill her position? She slipped up when I was out of the office, so now I don't think that I can put this on her."

I tried calming myself down, but it was no use. Jorge and I were being torn apart, yet again, and it still had to do with Ria.

"So every time something like this happens, you'll just up and fly away for who knows how long? And I'll be left behind like some chump?"

"Ginger, I love you so much, and I'm begging for your understanding. I have every intention of nipping this in the bud as soon as I get down there and then coming right back home. If there were any way of me getting out of this, believe me, I would. You are my only personal priority. But if I don't go, then I could lose my entire business."

I silently nodded while wiping away the tears streaming down my face.

How many times am I going to cry over this man?

"All right, well, I gotta go."

And before he could say a word, I hung up and rested my head on my closed laptop. It was still warm from all of the internet searching I had just done. Feeling utterly defeated, I realized that I needed to move on with my life. It was not what I'd been expecting, but I refused to be put on hold anymore.

I booted the laptop back up, went to my bank's first-time homebuyer's savings account information, and slid the fake engagement ring off my finger.

22

**Jorge
One Week Later**

It had been one week since I had last spoken with Ginger, and she had yet to return any of my phone calls. I always saw her car in its usual parking spot every morning as I was leaving for work. She started later than me, so I didn't think much of it. But I'd fought every urge not to pound on her door, begging for one more chance. If it had been any other woman ignoring me, no way would I have still been interested after a week of being ignored.

But Ginger was unlike any woman I'd ever dated before.

I hadn't consumed anything other than numerous cups of coffee and a bunch of protein bars since we last spoke. Whatever I was feeling was horrible, and I could only assume that it was depression. It was a feeling of not being complete because someone had suddenly abandoned you.

If this is what women go through every time a guy ghosts them, then I have a lot of apologizing to do.

I was in my office downtown that morning, exchanging emails with my private pilot about getting me down to Africa. He told me that we should go as soon as possible since a major storm was due to hit the coast any day now. The longer we waited, the higher the possibility of us getting caught in the storm became.

De Veers had sent me another email demanding to know how much longer it would be until someone met with the miners in Africa. I knew they were anxious to resolve the issue, as was I, but I could only do so much while running the company by myself. I told De Veers that I had to tie up a few loose ends in Miami before heading down there, which was total bullshit.

The truth was that I refused to leave Miami until Ginger started speaking with me again.

I sent her another text message that morning, and when she didn't reply, I tried calling her. She wasn't answering her cell or office phone, either. I started pacing back and forth in my office, causing several of my employees to watch me from the other side of the glass door.

Just send one of them to Africa, dammit!

I looked out the window, and sure enough, the clouds were starting to darken. If my pilot was right, this wasn't going to be a quick storm either. We were officially heading into hurricane season, and that meant that flying anywhere needed to be done right away. I sent one last text message to Ginger, waited five minutes for a reply, and then shoved my phone back into my pocket.

I couldn't postpone my trip any longer.

I practically peeled out of the parking lot and headed to the Lavender Dreams Spa. Confronting anyone at their place of work was something I never did, but this was an emergency. To me, anyway.

The smell of lavender hit me as soon as I walked inside, and I was surprised at how calm it instantly made me feel. That was until Eva came out to greet me.

"Jorge, it's so good to see you!"

"Yes, I need to speak with Ginger, please. Is she in her office?"

She looked confused. "No, she's been working from home all week. I haven't been able to get a hold of her, though. I'm surprised she didn't tell you."

"Wait, did you just say that you can't get a hold of her either?"

Eva shook her head, and it hit me just how bad I'd hurt Ginger by having to leave the country.

"I don't believe this," I said while pacing back and forth in front of the front desk.

Yuslan came out a few minutes later. "Is everything all right out here? Jorge, why do you look so stressed?"

If there were anyone who could give me some much-needed advice, it was Yuslan. He pulled me into his office.

"I had no idea that Ginger was working from home all week, Yuslan."

He nodded while handing me a cup of Cuban coffee.

"Did something happen between the two of you? And be honest, Jorge. You should know by now that I can tell when people are lying."

"Well, kind of, Yuslan. There's a miner's strike in Africa. I have to go down there for a while to fix everything and try to get the miners back on the job. Normally I'd send Ria, but she's out of the picture. Anyway, when I told Ginger, it upset her, and she hasn't spoken to me since. And I can't say that I blame her either."

"Why don't you have someone else that can go instead of you? If you fired Ria and that was her job, it seems to me that you have to fill that position."

"That's the thing, Yuslan. Ria screwed me so badly that I don't think I can ever trust anyone ever again."

He shook his head while folding his hands across his lap. "Jorge, only a foolish business owner would try to juggle everything at once. You can't handle every aspect of your business!"

"I know, Yuslan, but what else can I do? That woman robbed me of nearly a million dollars!"

He looked me up and down while smiling. "Something tells me that you're doing just fine without that, Jorge. A million dollars to you is probably fifty or a hundred bucks to the average working American." His cheesy words of wisdom made me chuckle, and I realized he was right.

I felt my face flush at bit. "Well, I suppose that's true. But I can't think of anyone to take Ria's position right now. I need someone with a strong work ethic that I can trust. Knowledge of the diamond industry would be a plus, but not necessary. It's really just basic human resources and accounting."

"That's what Ginger does here, Jorge. She's our accountant and takes care of human resources."

"Yes, and she loves her job here. I could never ask her to quit just to work with me, especially after the hell I've put her through these past few weeks."

Yuslan leaned forward and put both of his hands on my shoulders. "Jorge, arrangements can easily be made. There are ways around this, you know. Maybe she can work part-time for the salon remotely while taking care of the miner's strike. Or perhaps we'll give her a temporary leave of absence."

"No," I said while defiantly shaking my head. "It's not just having her switch jobs, Yuslan. She loves it here. You should see her face light up when she talks about the Lavender Dreams Spa. This is her family. I would never take that away from her."

"As part of her family, I am ordering you to offer Ginger the job until you find a suitable replacement. You know you want to offer it to her. The second I heard that Ria quit, I knew that you'd want Ginger in that position. And the fact that you don't want her to leave her family here, at the salon, proves to me that you are a man now, Jorge."

Listening to Yuslan speak was like having a heart-to-heart with your father, minus all of the guilt. There was something about him that understood things that were left unsaid.

"Are you sure, Yuslan?"

He stood up and wrapped his arms around me. "Of course, I'm sure, Jorge. Just remember to invite my wife and me to your wedding."

I chuckled at his comment. "But we're not even engaged, Yuslan."

He winked at me as we walked back to the reception area.

By the time I got to Ginger's condo, I had an entire speech in my head. The longer I pounded on her door, begging her to answer it, the more of it I forgot.

Ginger finally opened the door and let me inside. "What do you want, Jorge?"

"I know you're upset about me going to Africa, but I have an idea. What if you went with me?"

My offer did not sit well with her.

"Why on earth would I go to Africa with you, Jorge? This isn't a romantic vacation for us! You're going there on business."

I took her hand and led her to the couch, where we sat down next to each other. "Please hear me out, Ginger. I went to the spa and spoke with Yuslan."

"Why were you at the spa?"

"Because I couldn't leave for Africa without hearing from

you first. You have no idea how much pain I've been in this past week, without hearing your voice or seeing your face. Anyway, Yuslan suggested that you do Ria's old job until I find someone else to do it."

"Are you kidding me, Jorge? First, you ask me to be your fake fiancée, then we nearly go through with a fake wedding ceremony, and now you want me to do Ria's job?"

When she puts it that way, I can see why she's so upset.

"I know that the spa is like an extended family for you, Ginger, but Yuslan said they're more than willing to work everything out."

"You asked Yuslan before me? What is wrong with you?"

I held up my hands, desperate to calm her down. "Oh, God, no! No, Ginger. That's not what happened at all. I went there to beg you to talk to me, and Yuslan is the one who suggested that you do the job."

Her face started to soften.

"There's no way in hell that I'd ever ask you to do such a thing! I told him I could never ask that of you because of how much you love your working there!"

"Well, I appreciate you not being the one to mention me leaving first. But as much as I love you, Jorge, it's been nothing but stress ever since we got together. I mean, our time in Paris was amazing, but we're right back to square one."

"I know. Why don't you think about it and call me in the morning?"

Ginger nodded and walked me to the door, where I left

without either one of us saying another word. And by the time I got back to my downtown office, it hit me: she wasn't wearing the ring anymore.

23

Ginger

That night I tossed and turned in bed trying not to think about Jorge and me in Africa, working together to insure the miners were doing their job safely. I imagined how impressed Jorge would be with my negotiating abilities too. Finally falling asleep, I dreamed he would propose in some special way to me.

I woke up, gasping for air right as I was about to answer him.

I was aware Jorge needed an answer about Africa right away, and I wasn't prepared for that kind of pressure, which was odd, since I'd always worked well under the gun. But he was asking me to uproot my life for who knew how long, walk away from a job that I was in love with, and live in another country for possibly a few months.

As I watched the waves crashing against the shore from my balcony, I wondered just how far I'd go for Jorge. This past year had been all about my becoming a strong, independent woman. And independent women didn't abandon their lives for some guy. But it had also been the year that I had gotten to know Jorge, and I didn't want to throw away our relationship. The problem was that so much was happening to me all at once, and I told myself that anyone else in my position would also be stressed out.

Deciding that Jorge would have to wait a little bit longer for an answer, I put the whole Africa situation in the back of my mind and went into work that morning.

"Good morning," Eva said as I walked through the door.

I tried my best to put on a happy face, but she saw right through my façade.

"You don't look so good, Ginger. What's wrong?"

I shrugged while sipping my coffee. "It's a long story that I can't get into right now. How are things with you?"

"Still single and lonely. I can't find any part-time jobs, either."

"Are you sure that you want another job, Eva? I know you're lonely, but that's a lot of commitment on your part. Even though you're single, really think before applying for a job."

I made my way into my office and tried to focus on work. Thankfully I enjoyed what I did for a living, so it kept my mind occupied for a while. But that quickly dissipated within an hour, and all I could think about was Jorge.

My phone kept ringing off the hook, emails were piling up, and several employees had come into my office with concerns they should have been able to deal with on their own. A few of them noticed that I wasn't my usual self, either, and said they would come back another time. That made me feel even worse, though.

By the time lunch rolled around, I knew I had to make a decision.

I sat outside with my sandwich and salad, listening to the seagulls and waves crashing against the ocean. If I went to Africa with Jorge, I would be saying goodbye to the Lavender Dreams Spa. It wouldn't be such a big decision if Jorge could have given me a time frame. I wanted to at least give Yuslan a head's up ahead of time for when they could expect my return. But if I decided to go with Jorge, it could be anywhere from a week up to a year.

There's no way in hell that I'll leave the spa that long.

Sure, Yuslan noted that I'd always have a place here. But it would only be a matter of time before they'd need to fill my position. My biggest fear was getting an email while I was in Africa that said, oops, we've hired someone to take your place. Thanks for your time with the company. Guadalupe and Yuslan had always made me feel like a daughter, but they had a business to run.

Guadalupe came out to join me, not saying a word as she sat down across the table. All she did was stare and smile at me as I nibbled away on my sandwich. I knew she was waiting for me to tell her everything about Jorge and Africa. Even though she and I hadn't discussed it, Yuslan undoubtedly told her everything after our talk.

"Oh, Guadalupe. Why did I ever get mixed up with Jorge in the first place? None of this would be happening if we'd just remained friends."

She shook her head at me while clicking her tongue. "It would have been impossible for the two of you just to remain friends, Ginger. You must know that by now."

I tilted my head at her while sipping my water. "I don't know about that, Guadalupe. Jorge is an attractive man who could get just about any woman he wanted, and I'm just some accountant who works at a spa. I think I just got lucky."

"Luck isn't what brought you two together, Ginger. Jorge chose to be with you." She always had a way of knowing exactly what to say. "Before he met you, Ginger, wasn't he a womanizer? One of those men who goes gallivanting with numerous women, hopping from one to the next, and barely remembering any of their names. But not you."

I thought about my relationship with Jorge and how much it had evolved over the past year. We didn't have a romantic start, that was for sure. Chase had passed me off to him at Paris's wedding last year because he had wanted to dance with Margo, and I found him to be utterly boring. But as I looked back at that night, I realized that I wasn't bored by him at all.

I was just obsessed with keeping Margo away from Chase.

"That's true. Jorge has been with many women, and just thinking about him sleeping with Ria makes my skin crawl."

She shook her head while putting her hand on top of mine. "Ria is out of the picture now, Ginger. You need to forgive him for his past mistakes and look toward the future. That woman could throw herself naked at Jorge, and he'd probably run away screaming. He's with you now—only you."

I chuckled while picturing that scenario, knowing that Guadalupe was probably right. "As much as I love Jorge, Guadalupe, I can't go to Africa! I love my job here, and you just gave me a huge raise. You guys are like a family to me."

"Ginger, you forget the most important thing about families. No matter what comes between them, they're bound by love. Sure, there are moments when your family gets on your nerves, and you want nothing to do with them. For example, when Yuslan conveniently forgets to take out the garbage and I'm stuck doing that job."

I giggled as she complained about her husband. They were two peas in a pod and were adorable even when they bickered.

"But you'll have to have someone else do my job while I'm gone, Guadalupe. I can't tell you how much work I have to do. In fact, I should have had a working lunch hour instead of sitting out here. It'll require someone doing it at least forty-hours per week."

Guadalupe rolled her eyes at me while smiling. "That's for me to worry about, Ginger. The sooner you get your ass to Africa, the sooner you can return and have your job back. We'll probably just hire a temporary person, anyway."

I felt better knowing they'd go with a temporary employee instead of filling the job while I was gone, then having to move that poor person into another position.

"Do they even have temps who specialize in accounting?"

"You can get a temp for just about anything nowadays. I'm sure there's someone with your degree just looking for a position, who is registered with a temp agency. If they do a good job, maybe I'll create a position just for them to sign on. But again, Ginger, all that matters is that you accompany Jorge to Africa."

The more Guadalupe spoke about her plans for filling my position, the better I felt about the whole ordeal. I honestly had no problem leaving Miami for a while. Margo was busy with Chase and the baby, and Eva would soon be occupied with a part-time job...or boyfriend.

"Are you sure, Guadalupe? Because Jorge doesn't even know how long we'll be gone. If they're requiring him to visit the diamond mine, then I'm assuming it'll be longer than a month."

"Yes, dear. You know how I feel about alto, oscuro y guapo men! Now go tell Jorge that you'll go to Africa with him."

I grabbed my food and rushed back to my desk, eager to finish all of my work so that I could break the good news to Jorge.

The rest of the afternoon went by quickly, and I was able to get all of my work done by four o'clock. I had considered texting Jorge that I'd agreed to go with him to Africa but decided to surprise him at the office.

It was his usual night to work late, so on my way to his downtown office, I picked up his favorite kind of sushi and a bottle of white wine. I had put my engagement ring back on, too, and giggled whenever someone complimented its beauty. Even the cashier at the sushi restaurant said she'd never seen something quite as exquisite before, and when she asked when we were getting married, I simply said that we hadn't set a date yet.

By the time we get back from Africa, though, I'll probably be officially engaged.

Knowing how much he loved the French pastries in Paris, I picked up a box at a local bakery. I knew Jorge had repeatedly said that nothing in Miami was nearly as good as what we had eaten in Paris, but it was the next best thing. I also picked him up a chocolate-covered sugar cookie in the shape of a heart, hoping it would ease any tension between us. Even though I was right in standing my ground, I didn't want anything to get in the way of us being together anymore.

My heart was racing a mile a minute as I made my way up to his floor. The past week had been a living hell for me. As much as I loved and cared about Jorge, I had to stand my ground. But the further apart we were from each other, the more depressed I became, and I began to realize what it felt like to really be in love with someone. I had even come close to calling him a few times, but I was unsure of myself.

Once again, however, I had Yuslan and Guadalupe to thank for showing me the light. They were a couple who proved that anything was possible when you truly loved each other.

I rode the elevators up to his floor, my feet practically shaking in their shoes. If everything went according to plan that night, Jorge and I would be making love on his office desk.

Phew, it's hot in this elevator.

The elevator doors opened to his floor, and I was thrilled to see all of his employees gone for the day. That meant that it would definitely just be the two of us in his office, feeding each other sushi and French pastries, sipping white wine, and then running our hands all over each other like wild animals.

As I turned the corner toward his office, I noticed a pair of black high heels standing in front of his desk.

Please let that be his secretary.

Curious to hear what they were saying, I practically tiptoed to his door, careful not to make any sudden movements. And I had every intention of doing that until I reached his door, too, until I got a full look into his office.

The bottle of wine and cartons of sushi slipped out of my hands as my mouth fell open. Chardonnay seeped onto the pink marble floor as I saw Ria in his office, leaning across Jorge's desk as she spoke. It was impossible to see his face, but she was dressed to seduce in a tight red dress.

The sound of the wine bottle breaking caused both of them to turn around. Jorge jumped up from his desk while Ria smirked at me.

I flew down the stairs instead of taking the elevator, ignoring his pleas to stop the entire way down.

I am never falling in love again!

Walking in high heels had never been easy for me, but I practically ran in them toward my car. Jorge's feet were speeding up, but I got into my car before he could catch me. The tears were falling down my face so fast that I could barely see. I heard him screaming my name as I revved the engine and peeled out of the parking lot.

"Screw you, Jorge Stein!" I said it so loud at the first traffic light that the woman in the car next to me looked over. But I didn't give a shit.

I should have known they'd get back together! He probably saw her at The Spicy Pineapple and was turned on by her, then thought he'd sneak in a little after-work action! I can't believe I bought all of his lies!

I ripped my heels off while walking into my condo, where I promptly shut the door and locked it. I knew Jorge would probably be banging on my door later on, but at the rate I was going, I'd be fast asleep by the time that happened. I couldn't remember the last time I had cried so hard.

Before taking off all of my clothes and getting into bed, I powered off my phone. There were several missed calls and text messages from Jorge.

But that didn't matter anymore.

I had no choice but to cry myself asleep, regretting the day I ever laid eyes upon Jorge Stein.

24

Ginger

I woke up the next morning feeling worse than the night before. All night long, I had dreamed about Jorge. The two of us were back in Paris, taking romantic walks on the streets of Champs-Élysées and the Place de la Bastille. We enjoyed French pastries and cappuccinos outside, as people walked by and asked us when we were getting married. Jorge always held up my hand to show off the ring, and right before giving them a date, Ria showed up.

Ria, with her fake body and even faker personality. But even though Jorge professed that he was no longer attracted to her, especially after so much plastic surgery, I knew she could easily pass as a supermodel. She had a body that every woman pined for, and a face that had been sculpted to perfection. Sure, anyone could tell that it was all plastic. But she was still pretty.

The last dream I had was of her in Jorge's office, in the same scenario as I'd caught them in the night before. She was wearing the same outfit and leaning across the desk in the same manner. Only this time, I caught them right as they kissed.

It would have been easy to just stay in bed all day, refusing to acknowledge that I was single once again. But as I stared at my antique alarm clock, with its intricate ticking hands, I knew that I'd have to get out of bed. I leaned over to turn off the alarm portion, and that's when I saw it—the engagement ring.

It was breathtaking.

I leaned closer to get a better look at the diamond, and as I was squinting, I let out a massive sigh.

You need to move on with your life.

I ripped back the covers and forced myself out of bed. After waking up with some coffee, I ignored the growing depression within me and sat down at my desk. Jorge might be out of my life for good this time, but at least I still had my job down at the spa. The first thing on my agenda was to email Guadalupe, briefly explain the situation, and tell her that I'd be working from home that day.

All it took was my typing out the title of the email in order for the tears to start flowing. One hour and dozens of wadded-up tissues later, I finished composing a five-line email that basically said Jorge and I were over, and I wouldn't be leaving the spa.

Before hitting send, I contemplated checking my phone just to see what Jorge's excuse had been for last night. Right as I was about to turn the phone on, my doorbell rang.

I can't believe he has the balls to show his face here!

"Go away, Jorge! You must have me mistaken for Ria! I never want to see or speak to you again!"

"It's Yuslan. May I come inside?"

"Oh, sorry, Yuslan. Yes, one second." I quickly composed myself in the mirror, doing my best to make my reddened face look as though I hadn't been crying.

Screw it.

After saving the email to my drafts folder, I threw on a robe and let the man I considered to be my second father inside.

And right behind him walked Jorge.

"I thought I told you to leave, Jorge Stein!"

Yuslan held up his hands, and his calm disposition slowly lowered my blood pressure. "Ginger, you have every right to be upset with this man. But he has to tell you something." Yuslan turned to Jorge and nodded his head.

I leaned against my living room wall with my arms folded across my chest.

This ought to be good.

"Ginger, if I were you, I'd be just as angry. But please listen to my explanation!"

"I don't see what the point is, but go ahead, Jorge."

He let out a sigh before speaking. "When Ria heard about the De Veers diamond strike, she thought it'd be an easy way for her to get her job back. She knows how complex and demanding her position is, and that it would be incredibly difficult to find someone else on such short notice."

"If you think that I'm going to stay with you while that bitch is working for you again—"

Yuslan put his hand on my elbow and casually walked me over to my couch.

Jorge waited for me to sit down before proceeding. "Ria was also terrified of going to jail after getting paperwork from my lawyer. Obviously, I told her there wasn't a chance in hell that she could ever work for me again. That's when she promised to never make another sexual advance on me, hoping that would change my mind."

I rolled my eyes in disgust. "Yeah, Ria looked really professional while leaning across your desk with her breasts in your face!"

Yuslan held his hands up again. "Ginger, please let Jorge finish."

All right, but only because you're a good judge of character.

"That was nothing but bad timing," Jorge said. "And I'd completely forgotten to have the locks changed before we went on vacation. Please, Ginger. You have to believe me!"

I started to relax a little bit, remembering that he'd also forgotten about the email from the De Veers Diamond Group. The same one that had he checked it before we went to Paris, we wouldn't be stuck in this predicament in the first place.

"Anyway," Jorge continued, "I had her removed from the property as soon as you left. I was actually reaching into my pocket to get my cellphone when you walked in, just to have the cops show up. My lawyers are taking care of the whole Ria situation, and let's just say that if she comes within a thousand feet of me, she'll be spending a lot of time in jail. And that's in addition to the whole embezzling fiasco."

I looked over at Yuslan, who was smiling at me while holding my hand.

"Jorge is a good man, Ginger, who just got mixed up with a very bad woman."

Tears started welling up in the corners of my eyes as our gazes met. Jorge looked just as stressed out as I'd been over the past twelve hours. I jumped up off of the couch and wrapped my arms around him.

"Oh, I'm so sorry, Jorge! I should have waited for an explanation! It's just that with everything going on these past few weeks, I didn't know what to think. So, Ria's really gone for good this time?"

He reached into his pocket and showed me some paperwork, which proved that Ria wasn't allowed anywhere near his business or himself. "Ria's really gone for good, Ginger. It's just the two of us now."

"I don't know what to say, Jorge."

He ran a hand through my long, auburn hair while staring deeply into my eyes. "Say that you'll come with me to Africa, Ginger. I don't know how long I'll be down there, but I can't go without you by my side. I know that I'm asking you to leave the job of your dreams, along with your friends and family, but I promise that it's not a permanent move. Our home will always be here in Miami."

Hearing him say "our" home made my knees weak.

I looked at Yuslan, who nodded while smiling at me.

"Go to Africa with Jorge, Ginger. He needs you more than we do at the spa right now. But you'll have to leave today because the sooner you do, the sooner you'll be back with your family at the Lavender Dreams Spa."

I turned to Jorge as my jaw dropped in surprise. "Today, Jorge? We have to leave today?"

He glanced at his watch and nodded. "I'm afraid so. We are in hurricane season now, and the weather is very unpredictable. So there is an opening today for us to shoot on over to Africa, and my pilot is on standby. How quickly do you think you can pack your bags?"

"Well, that depends on how long we'll be gone. Which, as you pointed out, we have no way of knowing."

"Whatever you can't pack within an hour, I can always have shipped there. So, you're definitely coming with me to Africa?"

I nodded while planting my lips onto his, thankful to have the man of my dreams back in my life where he belonged. I hadn't planned on kissing him for so long, but our emotions got the better of us.

After several minutes of kissing, Yuslan quietly saw himself out.

I had never packed so quickly before in my life. Since I'd be working for Jorge's company, I packed every work outfit that would fit in my suitcases along with toiletries. As I grabbed my passport out of the safe, I sent a quick text message to Eva, asking if she'd mind getting my mail while I was gone.

Eva: Of course! Would you mind if I stayed at your place, too?

Me: Go for it!

Eva: Thank you! It'll be like a mini vacation. Plus, your condo is so much nicer than my apartment!

Going to Africa would benefit both Eva and me because I knew just how lonely she'd been ever since she broke up with her last boyfriend.

In what seemed like only a few minutes, Jorge's driver showed up ready to take us to the airport, where his private aircraft flew us to Africa. Both of us slept for most of the trip, emotionally exhausted over the past several weeks.

***

Jorge had made reservations at a five star hotel with breathtaking views in Kimberly, South Africa. That night, we had made love all night long and had a romantic breakfast the following morning at a local restaurant. And that's when I saw that something was missing from my left hand.

"Oh, shoot. I left the ring back at my condo. It would

have been fun pretending we were engaged here, too, just like we did in Paris."

"Yeah, that was a lot of fun, wasn't it? I especially loved how much your face lit up every time someone asked when we were getting married."

I shrugged nonchalantly, even though I loved where the conversation was headed. "Well, you know me. I've always been good at pretending to be a fake bride."

"Actually, I'm kind of glad that you left it behind."

I tried containing my excitement while acting aloof, but inside I was a ball of nerves. "Why do you say that, Jorge?"

He got down on one knee and looked up at me while smiling. "I think you know why I'm saying that, Ginger. It's because you are the only woman I want to be with for the rest of my life. I suppose I knew that shortly after we started talking every week, and everything solidified after our first night together."

Tears were streaming down my face a mile a minute, but I didn't say a word as he continued.

"Yuslan was right about something, too. He told me that finding the perfect woman is what defines a man, and that's exactly how I feel about you. Before we became more than friends, Ginger, I was lost. I can't imagine my life without you. So with that being said, will you marry me?"

"Yes, Jorge! I'll marry you!"

Everyone in the diner burst out in a round of applause.

"I'll take you to the mines later on, and you can pick out

your very own diamond in the rough. I'll have it cut however you like, and then we'll fit it on a platinum band."

"Oh, Jorge! I'm so excited!"

"That's what I was going for, Ginger. I don't want there to be any secrets between us anymore."

"Well, in that case, I should come clean about something. I lost my birth control when they were looking through my bags at customs. I should have told you last night before we made love, but I couldn't resist. I'm so sorry."

He brushed some hair out of my face while smiling. "Oh, well. All that matters is that we love each other and make the commitment to spend the rest of our lives together. And, of course, the next thing for us to do is start a family."

EPILOGUE

Ginger
Eighteen Months Later

Brooks was having so much fun in the tub that morning. I still couldn't believe that he was mine and Jorge's son, but his crystal-blue eyes were definitely from his father. Guadalupe said that he had my eyebrows and lips, though. Every time I looked at him, all I saw was a bouncing baby boy created by two people who were soulmates.

Ever since I was a little girl, my dream home had included a full bathroom attached to every bedroom—even the guest rooms. And that was precisely what Jorge had done with our newly constructed mansion, which was just a few blocks away from Chase and Margo. Baby Brooks had a nursery that was twice the size of my childhood bedroom and an attached bathroom complete with a soaker tub and walk-in shower. Until he was a few months older, however, I bathed him in his bathroom sink.

My cellphone started ringing, and before Jorge even brought it to me, I knew it was Guadalupe.

"Put it on speakerphone," I said while rinsing off Brooks.

"Is that Brooks I hear splashing away, Ginger?"

Brooks cooed and giggled upon hearing her voice.

"It sure is, Guadalupe! I'll be heading to work in just a few minutes. Brooks got a little too carried away with his breakfast, and needless to say, I had to give him a bath."

"You take all of the time that you need, dear. I only called because your messenger said that you weren't available, and I wanted to hear him. Will you send me some pictures this afternoon?"

Guadalupe had pictures of Brooks all over her office, right next to Margo's baby, Joanna. Even though we weren't blood-related to her, she was still their grandmother.

"Of course, I will! Although I don't think you'll have too much room left on the walls!"

"Let me worry about that, dear. If I need to, I'll have Yuslan make my office bigger."

Jorge burst out laughing while bringing me a towel for my wet baby. "That poor man is always working at the spa."

"Believe me, Jorge, I repay him with plenty of home-cooked meals. Speaking of which, when are you two coming over for some of my empanadas?"

"Oh, God, Guadalupe, I could go for some of your delicious empanadas right now! How about this weekend?" I asked.

"Sure, but only if Jorge can wait that long!"

"Guadalupe," Jorge said while continuing to dry off Brooks, "you won't hear me complaining if you bring me some of your delicious cooking. Just be sure to bring more than one serving because Ginger will get to it before I do!"

"It's not my fault that you're slow," I said while kissing him. Both of us looked down at our son, who kept giggling as the two of us rubbed him with a towel.

I have never felt this happy in my life.

I dressed Brooks in an outfit I had received at my baby shower and sat him down on his play mat in my home office. It was directly in front of my desk, where I had been working ever since I'd had him. Guadalupe had encouraged me to take a more extended maternity leave, but I loved my job too much. Between Jorge and me working from home, we were more than able to take care of Brooks in between getting stuff done. Besides, he was a pretty easy baby. As long as he had his toys, we could get our work done.

As Brooks rolled around on his play mat, I snapped a few pictures for Guadalupe.

"You are such a beautiful baby!"

I sent the pictures to Guadalupe via our interoffice instant messaging system and then took a few moments to look at the pictures on my desk.

While in Africa, it hadn't taken me long to help Jorge

negotiate with the miner's union. So we had returned to Miami within six weeks of our departure. And a few months later we had married. Most of the pictures on my walls and in my phone were of Jorge and me on our wedding day.

At the time, my baby bump had been relatively small, and I'd hoped nobody would notice. But Guadalupe noticed within seconds of seeing me in the gown. So did Margo and Eva. Thankfully, they kept the news to themselves until Jorge and I were ready to tell everyone.

I found myself doubled over with laughter as I remembered how Guadalupe kept making subtle references about my small, baby bump that night. If I hadn't known any better, I'd say she was more excited about the baby than we were.

Brooks was rolling back and forth on the mat, his tiny body reaching for the occasional stuffed animal as he made the most adorable baby sounds. I scooped him up and held him to my chest, secretly wondering how much longer it'd be until we had another baby. Jorge and I hadn't discussed that yet, but our mansion was big enough to expand our family. I couldn't wait until we had a house full of children running around and playing while Jorge and I lived our best lives.

Jorge brought me a cup of freshly brewed coffee a few minutes later, and then sat down on the mat with Brooks. I watched them play for as long as I could before opening up my laptop and resuming my work. Once again, the emails were piling up, but I was someone who thrived under pressure. And even though I knew Jorge wouldn't mind if I quit working, the truth was that I couldn't see not having a job. In addition to taking care of Brooks, it gave me a sense of purpose in life.

Right as I was finishing up, Eva came over with some of our favorite coconut lattes. The smell wafted into my office.

"Oh, Eva, thank you! Gosh, I could eat nothing but coconut all day long!"

Eva sat down on the other side of the playmat, and I watched as both she and Jorge played with Brooks. She was still single and looking, both for a boyfriend and a part-time job. Having Brooks gave her more reasons to stop over to visit, though, and that made me happy. If Jorge and I didn't work from home all of the time, we would have easily hired her as a nanny.

"You're welcome. I cannot handle how cute Brooks is, you guys! And Jorge, he looks just like you!"

Jorge winked at me, knowing that would get under my skin a little bit.

"You know, Eva, I'm the one who gave birth to him!"

She chuckled while playing with Brooks's tummy. "Oh, I know. Brooks looks like you, too. His face is almost identical to Jorge's!"

It was hard arguing with her because one look at Brooks, and it was apparent that Jorge was his father.

"You are so good with children, Eva. Just look at the way Brooks's face lights up every time you nuzzle him!"

Eva giggled while holding our son, then pressed her face against his. She loved him just as much as Jorge and I did.

"That's just because he's the sweetest little boy there ever was!"

"Anyway, how are things at your condo?"

"You mean *your* condo?"

Shortly after Jorge and I had returned from Africa, I had moved into his penthouse and sublet my condo to her. My name was still on the lease, of course, but she had full control over the space. She had turned my former home office into a guest bedroom, too.

"It's yours now, Eva. In fact, when it comes time to renew the lease, I'm more than happy to recommend you to the property manager."

"That's a great idea, thank you! I absolutely love it there, you guys. The views are phenomenal, and just like you did, Ginger, I watch the ocean every morning while sipping my coffee. The only thing missing is...well, you know."

I sighed while thinking about how lonely Eva must have been. Jorge gave her a sympathetic look, too. She had never been someone who did well on her own. If Eva weren't in a relationship, then she wasn't happy. And the men she'd been casually dating were nothing but jerks who treated her like an object.

"It'll happen when the timing is right, Eva. I'll keep my eyes open for anyone who looks worthy enough of being called your boyfriend too. Just keep telling yourself that, all right?"

Jorge interjected, "Me too, Eva. Unfortunately, all of the guys I work with are not interested in a lasting relationship."

I chuckled while leaning back in my chair. "That's because you used to be one yourself."

He held up his hands while shrugging. "Hey, if I could change my past, I would in a heartbeat. Except for the part where you and I get together, that is."

Eva rolled her eyes as Jorge and I kissed. "Get a room, you two. On second thought, why don't you go to your room while I watch Brooks?"

I laughed while shaking my head. "We can wait, Eva."

She giggled while continuing to play with Brooks, who was delighted at seeing one of his aunts again. They looked so cute together, and I couldn't help but think what a wonderful mother Eva would be one day.

"I just wish I didn't have so much free time. There are only so many movies I can watch at home before I go stir-crazy." The doorbell rang, and Jorge went to answer it. "Take last night, for example. There was a back-to-back romcom feature on television, and even after it was over, I still couldn't sleep. Ugh, I just hate sleeping alone. You're so lucky, Ginger."

Gavin poked his head into my office, and Eva's eyes instantly lit up. "Hello, I'm Gavin."

"Hi, I'm Eva."

I took Brooks out of her arms, thereby allowing her to shake Gavin's hand. There was no denying the spark between them, either.

"It's a pleasure to meet you." He turned to me and smiled. "Is that Brooks?" Gavin took him from me, and once again, Brooks was elated to see another face.

"That boy just eats up attention," I said while sitting back down in my chair.

Gavin walked back and forth, carrying Brooks, smiling from ear to ear.

"Gosh, I miss having my daughter. She was so cute at this age. They're just so cute and cuddly, you know? When they get older, watch out Ginger: they love to run all over the house. I can't tell you how many times I've had to chase after my little girl while she giggled and ran away from me."

Eva and I laughed while Gavin continued playing with Brooks.

"Anyway," I said to Ginger, "I'll be sure to keep my eyes and ears open if I hear of any part-time job openings."

Gavin's eyes lit up as he turned to face Eva. "Did you say that you're looking for a part-time job?"

"Yes, I am. I work at the Lavender Dreams Spa with Ginger and Margo, but I have plenty of time on the nights and weekends."

"Really? Because I'm in desperate need of a babysitter."

Made in the USA
Las Vegas, NV
08 July 2021